Love
Have Mercy
2

by

Kordarow Moore

Love Have Mercy 2

ISBN: 978-1-7366158-4-3

About the Author

Kordarow Moore is a 31-year-old male born in Chicago, Illinois and raised in Madison, Wisconsin. He is the fifth born child of six by Marguerite and Kevin Moore. He has a daughter named Korvaya Moore who is his pride and joy. Kordarow Moore has been incarcerated for nine years in a federal prison for distribution of narcotics. He is on his final year of an 11-year sentence. While incarcerated, he's tried to learn as much as possible about accounting, marketing, real estate, and business management. Upon his release, he plans to pursue a career in accounting and investing. Also, he plans to do some motivational speaking to the inner-city youth who are experiencing some of the same struggles that he did while growing up in poverty. He's currently working on two more romance fiction books with Bagz Of Money Content. So, be on the lookout for more from Kordarow Moore.

Table of Contents

Love Have Mercy on Me 2

Prologue

This is Louis, here to bring you up to date on where everyone's life so far. As you might remember, I finally found someone who could keep up with me. Cante was so different from the women I was used to dating. I'm an ex-player, yet Cante decided to give love a chance for the first time, just like me. Things were going really well up until her visit to my condo in New York where she found me there with my little sister, Jhanell. She allowed her old trust issues to arise and thought I was cheating, which made her run away. I couldn't focus with things being the way they were between us and couldn't think about anything else but her. I decided to hire my trusted private investigator who gave me her location. That's when I showed up in Tijuana at her photo shoot.

"That's it Cante, that's the pose that I'm looking for right there. No, slightly tilt your head to the right. Exactly, Cante, perfect! That's perfect!" shouted the photographer, excited to have her.

Cante was in her element. This was her place to be, free from the world and all its problems. At her photo shoots, she focused on nothing but herself and embraced the environment that felt like Elysia. She stood tall while posing, looking fabulous in the foreign garb that hugged her curves. Her hair was tied up in a tight bun that helped highlight her beautiful facial features.

The photographer continued to shout directions. "Now, turn your head left and rest your hands above your head. That's exactly what I'm looking for, perfect. Cante, perfect!" The photographer continued to snap away as Cante closed her eyes, reveling in the moment. She continued to free her mind from all the things surrounding her life; especially her situation involving me. Every time she thought about what she was going through, it brought a sharp pang to her heart. She continued to pose with the ferocity and determination of someone who refused to break under pressure. She not only wanted to look stronger, she wanted to fit the part as well.

She opened her eyes and was taken aback by the sight before her. I stood next to the photographer standing tall while peering into her. Cante's heart skipped a beat and a lump the size of an orange formed inside of her throat. She watched the photographer bring the camera down as I leaned into him so I could whisper into his ear. "Everyone take twenty, please."

All the patrons in the room began to file out, but Cante stayed in place. She couldn't move if she wanted to as the sight of me had her in a trance. She watched nervously as I approached her, feeling her heart pick up and the butterflies in her stomach floating recklessly around.

"Hey Cante," I said while standing in front of her. Cante cast her glance down at the ground without responding. She didn't want her response to come out feeble. She wanted to display the same strength and resilience she felt earlier while posing, but it was hard for her. My strong presence, hard stare and controlled demeanor were what made her weak to me. "How'd you find me, Louis?"

"I have my ways, Cante," I replied in my deep baritone voice. Silence overtook the place as we both tried finding the right words.

"Cante," I started again, "On my way over here, I contemplated having a million bouquets of roses to arrive. I also thought about purchasing you some of the most expensive pieces of jewelry that I could find. I did neither. I came here today, not bearing gifts, but bearing my heart because that's the most important thing I have to give to you." I looked into Cante's eyes with extreme desire and longing.

"Cante, I need you to understand this is all new to me. I'm not sure if I'm doing it perfectly or if I'm making a complete fool out of myself. What I do know is that I can't control myself. Cante, I can't control the lonely feeling that invades my heart when I'm missing you. I can't... I can't control the crazy thoughts that have been forming inside of my mind when I think of losing you." I paused again while trying to regain my composure, choking up and fighting to keep the tears from falling.

"Cante, there isn't another woman on this planet that could lead me to betray you. I need you to know and understand that I don't want or need another woman but you. I'm in love with you, Cante, and that's how I feel for the very first time in my life."

Cante looked into my eyes trying to find a sign of deception. After finding none, she began to speak. "Louis I have to admit to you that I'm scared. I'm so afraid to trust you with my heart. I'm afraid of getting played. I've witnessed a fool's pain before and it's nothing that I would like to experience."

Cante paused to allow her words to settle. "Louis, I've heard similar things from men who have lied and tried covering it up by appearing sympathetic. How do I know that you're not playing me, Louis? You know the game just as well as I, wasn't it always what it looked like?" Cante finished.

I took in Cante's words, knew they held validation, because I once held the same reservations. I understood the game in and out and knew that it could really end painfully if you wasn't careful. It was that knowledge that kept me from committing seriously for so long in the past.

"Cante, I have no intention of misleading you. If my intentions weren't to be loyal to you, I would've done to you what I've done to plenty of women before you, walk away once I was done. The reason that I'm standing here right now is because my intentions are to be with you. Believe it or not, Cante, that woman at my condo was one of the closest people that I have to family, and I apologize for not informing you of our history before. Cante, there was nothing sexual going on between us, and if it were, I would've been man enough to admit it to you. I understand your paranoia because it was once mine, but once I decided to give us a shot, I did so by leaving all insecurity behind me. I recognize that the only way that I can give myself a real shot at loving you is to trust you. I wouldn't lead you on or lie to you, Cante. I couldn't hurt you in that way. I need you to believe in me like I believe in you."

"Trust is a hard thing to gain Louis, but it's such an easy thing to lose" whispered Cante.

"Well, allow me to spend the remainder of my time regaining your trust 'cause I'll never

give you a reason to lose it" I assured her. I lifted her chin up in order for her to look into my eyes. "I love you, Cante Lightfeather. Trust me and believe in my love because it will never betray you."

Cante wrapped her arms around my neck. "Louis, I'll surrender myself to you, but please do not hurt me." With that said, she stood on her tippy toes and kissed me with all of her heart...

Okay, so y'all see your boy went and got what was his. That's only the beginning of my journey with Cante. Now, I know y'all are wondering what happened between my home boy Kyle and Zoe and also what happened between Arnold and Erica. Honesty, I initially thought Erica and Kyle would get back with one another, but I guess love had other plans. As you can remember, Kyle met Zoe who unexpectedly swept him off his feet, or better yet, they began to sweep one another off their feet. The timing of their union was perfect, Kyle needed Zoe and Zoe needed Kyle. At least that's what we thought before Kyle's indecisiveness caused him to go running from love again. But did he make it back to Zoe?

Zoe's excitement heightened once she felt the blindfold being lifted from her. She'd been stuck in a state of suspense ever since she was whisked away from a company meeting by several of her coworkers promising a pleasant surprise. Once the blindfold was lifted, she stood blinking continuously to regain focus. She noticed she was at the restaurant in South Korea where her and Kyle first went to eat.

"Zoe Fields, who everyone calls Zoe," she heard the familiar voice say. Zoe tensed up and felt a wave of goosebumps shoot through her body. She turned on her heels in a desperate attempt to see the man that captured her heart before disappearing with it just like a thief in the night.

"Kyle!" She shouted in both shock and surprise.

Kyle stood before her holding a single red rose in one hand and a red velvet jewelry box in the other. The wide smile plastered on his face caused Zoe's heart to flutter as she began to walk towards him. Once there, she looked into his eyes. "Where have you been, Mr. Malone?"

"I've been with you" Kyle responded. "I mean, not literally, but... I mean" Kyle stuttered as his nervousness showed clearly through his words. "What I mean is that my heart has been with you the entire time. I understand that the way I left our last night together wasn't the best way to go about it, I was inconsiderate, and I apologize to you for it. Today, I had you brought to me because I'm ready, Zoe. I'm done running. I'm done being afraid, and I'm done holding back. I'm ready to give you my all and to receive your all-in return. Zoe, every moment that we spent together helped me see that I've been in desperate need for what's within you. I need you in my life, Zoe, could you forgive me and give me the chance to do it right this time?"

Zoe looked into Kyle's eyes; he didn't need her forgiveness because she never felt forsaken.

She understood the battle that Kyle was having within. She herself had put her demons to rest and given herself a real chance to go out and experience love again. True, he could've handled it better, but he handled it just the way he needed to because it led him back to her. She missed him so much but stayed quietly in the background patiently awaiting their reunion; a union that she felt was destined to be.

"There's no reason for me to forgive you, Kyle. I understand what you were going through. I realized there was nothing I or no one else could do to get you to the place that you needed to be, only you could've done what you've done. I felt it in your touch within our last night spent together that love had prevailed."

Kyle looked into Zoe's eyes in both admiration and amazement. He felt like he was lucky to have such an understanding, compassionate, and wise woman holding the key to his heart.

"Zoe, I'm ready if you are" Kyle stated before holding out the red rose for Zoe to take along with the jewelry box.

Zoe brought the rose to her nose and inhaled its scent before opening the jewelry box to find the newest edition of a ladies Richard Millie watch inside. The gift made Zoe smile as she reached up and wrapped her arms around the neck before kissing him passionately on the lips. Kyle reciprocated her desire as he wrapped his arms around her waist, bringing her closer to him. The exchange began to get really heated. Someone shouted, "Get a room!" The remark caused them both to laugh.

"Take me away from here, Kyle. If I recall, you owe me another night" she told him.

"A night, you have me for the remainder of your life" replied Kyle before scooping Zoe up and carrying her away.

Damn, did the homie just say the remainder? I guess we'll just have to see how that turns out. Finally, we have Erica's relationship with Arnold. I know y'all remember that confusion that Erica faced between wanting to be with Arnold or with my homie, Kyle. Her confusion led to things getting crazy once the two men bumped heads at Kyle's condo. I don't really know Arnold, but I had to tip my hat to him for fighting for what and who he loved; not just with Erica, but for his father as well. His fight for his father is what led him into his encounter with Mr. Swiss and that's when things got crazy.

Arnold sat disoriented on the hardwood floor, sweating. He couldn't hear or see anything around him and felt as if he was having an out-of-body experience. The only sense he had of his heart beating wildly, the feeling of sweat dripping from his face and the feeling of the rubber grip pistol that he was holding. He released the gun from his grip like it was infected. Did he really? Had he just taken a life? *That couldn't be possible*, he thought to himself. He began to look around,

he looked for a sign of familiarity but found none. He tried making it to his feet, but the weakness that he felt within him wouldn't permit it.

"Dad!" He managed to scream out. "Dad! Where are you?" He began looking around for his father. "Dad!" he yelled out again before looking down at his hands. He noticed that his hands were covered in blood. The sight of all the blood made him panic even more. He didn't know where he was; he didn't know where his father was, all he did know was that he did something terribly wrong. Had he blanked out? Had he killed someone? *It couldn't be*, he thought to himself while trying to make it to his feet. He gathered himself and as he stood he staggered. He began wobbling around the nearly empty room, trying to find a sense of life. A sharp pain shot through his head and it brought him down to his knees. He brought his hands up to his head trying to stop the pain.

Mr. Swiss. The image of Mr. Swiss struck him. Was it... Mr. Swiss that he'd killed? He remembered seeing him, but where was he now? Was this his blood? Once the pain subsided in Arnold's head, he made it back to his feet. Stumbling, he made it to a doorway off to the side of the room. He looked in and saw blood all over the floor. He broke down to his knees and was hit with the same head pain from earlier, but worse. He tried opening his eyes, but couldn't. "Dad!" he managed to scream out again before forcing his eyes open.

This time, there was no mistaking what he'd seen at the end of the trail of blood. He began crawling on all fours, trying to make it to the deceased. With each crawl, the pain in his head intensified. He began to yell, he yelled out for the pain to stop, He yelled out begging for strength to get him over to the life that he'd taken. Finally, he doubled over. He began to cry. He cried long and hard sobs that echoed throughout the warehouse. He cried out of regret, pain, and sorrow. He didn't intend to hurt anyone. He wasn't violent by nature, but had found himself in a position where violence was necessary. Slowly, he turned himself around facing the lifeless body once again, the sight made him vomit. He began to think of his father and how someone once took his life. He'd always told himself that he wouldn't become the same monster as the person that killed his father; but now, he was. He reached inside his pocket in search of his phone. Once he located it, he dialed nine-one-one before putting it into his ear.

"Nine-one-one dispatch, what is your emergency?" asked the dispatcher.

"I've killed someone" replied Arnold.

"Can you please give me your location, and tell me who it is you've killed?"

"I... I... I don't know any location and can't see who it is exactly that I've killed, but I know I killed them," responded Arnold disoriented.

"What is your name, sir?"

"Arnold Lamount Simmons, Jr." responded Arnold. "You know what?" said Arnold after breaking from his reverie. "I'm not going to kill you and become the same monster you are, instead" said Arnold before pulling out his iPhone and speaking into it.

"Come on in" stated Arnold before ending the call. "I'm going to turn over this recording of you admitting to murder to a couple of my homicide contacts and allow them to serve their justice, you greedy piece of shit."

Just then, the abandoned warehouse was flooded with detectives. They approached the two as Arnold backed off. "Mr. Swiss, you are under arrest for the 1996 homicide of Arnold Lamount Simmons, Sr."

* * * * *

Erica sat on her bed with her legs crisscrossed, softly crying. She was in an almost complete state of panic with worry over Arnold. She found herself in this position almost daily since the dramatic scene that unfolded the night Arnold ran off. It had been over a week and she still hadn't heard from him.

She was sick with worry and couldn't figure out what to do. She began to rub her stomach as she thought about their child that she was carrying. She really hoped and prayed that he was okay and that he was just going through some things. She couldn't imagine something happening to him and having to be a widow raising a child alone. She began to cry even harder from these thoughts. She felt like she was beginning to lose her mind, so she took to talking to Cante and to her father and heeding their advice. They both had comforted her time and time again, that Arnold was okay and that he would be home the moment he got his mind together. She found a little peace from their words and felt like she knew that Arnold would never abandon her and their unborn child, but she worried, nevertheless. She leaned over and snatched the framed picture off the nightstand taken of them on their wedding day. She stared at it for a moment before whispering to herself "I hope that you're okay."

"I am" she heard a voice say.

She looked up and saw Arnold as he walked inside of their room, noticing her crying while holding their wedding picture. "Arnold!" screamed Erica before hopping from their bed and into his arm. "Oh my God! You're okay! You're okay!" she screamed as he held her tightly. "Where were you? What had happened? Are you okay?" The questions came one after another as her excitement took hold.

"I'm okay" he replied before taking Erica by the hand and sitting her down.

He began to tell her everything that had transpired. He told her how he'd first become suspicious of something being up with Mr. Swiss at the opening of `forever together' because every time he shook his hand, he got a sharp pain in his head and a vision of his father's face as well. He told her about the nightmare he'd had the night he ran from the house and how Mr. Swiss had admitted to having his father assassinated. He told her about how he'd flown out to California for a chance to clear his mind, and with doing so, he was able to devise the plan that had led to Mr. Swiss confessing to his role in his father's murder. After he finished, Erica just wrapped her arms around him and held him. She was happy to have him back home, safe and sound.

"I'm so sorry you had to go through all of that, I know how much your father means to you and I'm glad that you've been able to get a form of closure, I know how bad you needed it." she stated.

"You know I had a strong urge to take his life, but I understood that not only would I be the same as him. I'd be leaving my wife to raise a child alone and I couldn't imagine that. I made a promise to be here for the two of you and I'm keeping it" finished Arnold before kissing Erica gently as she closed her eyes to thank the heavens above. Now that you've been brought up to date on everyone's situation it's time to see what's to come.

Part 4

"I've resisted you, fought against you, and refused to fall victim to you. I've never believed in your powers and I've always thought of you as a myth. I've ignored you, brushed you off, played games with you, and even laughed from the mention of you. I didn't pay attention to the warnings of you arising, I just kept on moving through life as if your sudden appearance wasn't surprising. You've caught me off guard, love, entrapping me within your twisted web without any way to escape you. Why me, love? Why subject me to the hurt and heartache that you cause when I've never meddled with you? Is no one exempt from your onslaught? Is no one free from your wrath? Do you have mercy on anyone, love? If so, may you please have mercy on me too?"

-Cante Lightfeather

Chapter One

FOUR YEARS LATER

Arnold & Erica

"Mr. Simmons," began the civil judge in the packed courtroom. "The state of Minnesota as well as myself would like to offer you our deepest condolences for the unfortunate loss of your father so many years ago. We sympathize with the trauma you've faced and understand the effects that it had upon your life. So, today there will be another round of judgement passed down in this unfortunate case. Mr. Simmons, along with the life sentence that Mr. Swiss received for his involvement in your father's murder, the state of Minnesota would also like to grant you complete ownership of ten of Mr. Swiss' most lucrative companies beginning with the very company that caused so much heartache to begin with; Swiss Pharmaceuticals, including Swiss Hedge Funds, Swiss Homes Inc., Swiss Banks of Europe, Japan, China and the Virgin Islands, and last but not least, Swiss Accounts of Canada, South Korea, and the United States of America.

Now, Mr. Simmons, we understand that no amount of judgement could replace the loss of your father, but we hope that you feel that justice has been served. Again, we offer you our deepest condolences and wish you the best. Judgement has been passed down in this case, this court is now adjourned."

The foreboding sound of the gavel getting slammed gave the patrons in the courthouse permission to file out. Arnold exited and paused briefly atop the descending stairs and thought about the judgement that he'd just won. He looked forward to taking on acting control of the corporations. Two of the corporations he held a special interest in, the first was Swiss Pharmaceuticals because he felt he could live out his father's dream. The second was Swiss Accounts. The accounting firm brought him back memories of his encounter with Kyle, and the fact that he now owned the firm that Kyle worked for gave him a weird feeling of pleasure knowing that now he would have Kyle's career at his mercy. He hadn't seen or heard from Kyle since they encountered one another at Kyle's condo, but he hadn't forgotten about the disrespect Kyle shown towards his relationship with Erica. To him, Kyle would forever be an adversary and he would take advantage of any opportunity he had to bring Kyle down to his knees.

He quickly made it down the stairs of the courthouse and into his truck. Once inside, he sat back, closed his eyes and took several deep breaths. He began to think about his father. He knew that his father was looking down on him, watching his every move. It gave him a sense of fulfillment knowing that he had helped to solve his murder. He now felt that his father hadn't died in vain. He had plans to make his father proud, he now had the opportunity to show him that he'd raised a resilient and brilliant businessman. He would remove the name Swiss from all the corporations and change them to the name Simmons. He felt that these corporations were built on his blood, so it was only right that they held his name. He knew that, had his father not been murdered, his name would have been in the same conversation as Jeff Bezos, Tyler Perry, and Mark Zuckerberg. Instead, he was robbed of that opportunity. It had been ingrained in Arnold to

become a business tycoon and he was ready to take on the challenge. He opened his eyes, sat up straight, and started the engine to his car. Before pulling off, he told his Alexa to get Erica on the phone.

"Hey, honey" said Erica.

"Hey, I was calling to inform you that I was done in court and I'm on my way home. Do you need me to pick up anything from the store for you or baby Arnold?" he asked.

"No, we're okay. So, how'd it go today?" asked Erica rhetorically of the verdict. She'd already heard the results just as well as the rest of the world. The case was international news and had been broadcast on almost every news station.

"Okay, I guess" Arnold paused briefly before continuing. "I just really wish I had my father back."

Erica heard the pain in Arnold's voice and it made her feel bad for him. She knew that there was nothing she could do or say that would relieve his pain. She could only wish that she could take his pain away.

"I'm sorry" was the only thing that she could think to say. The phone became quiet for some time before Erica began speaking again. "Your son has been driving me crazy, I'm not sure where he gets all of the energy from, but it's too much for me" she vented.

The thoughts of his son turned his frown upside down before he even realized it. He was proud of the child they had together and looked forward to instilling into him the same morals, values, and strengths that his father had once instilled inside him. Their son was four years old now and seemed to be growing faster in the blink of an eye. Arnold spent as much time as he could with them, only allowing his business trips to California to interfere with their quality time. Now he knew that, since he'd won the verdict, his trips to California wouldn't be the only thing interfering.

As if Erica could read his mind, she said in a serious tone. "Honey, I understand your goals, dreams and ambitions, so I know that it's about to dive headfirst into your new responsibilities. I just want you to know that we fully support you and we understand that your time at home will become limited. We want you to do what you have to do, and we will continue to value every minute of the time that you are home with us" she finished supportively.

Her show of support really warmed Arnold's heart. These were the times that helped him see that he'd chosen the right woman to marry. At times it was like she could read into his deepest thoughts and fears. She gave him a peace like no other. Oftentimes she ended his worries before they had a chance to take effect. Behind every man was a strong woman and she was reminding him that he was a king of their castle and that his queen and prince would always be awaiting him.

"Thank you for always being understanding, but now I need you to put baby Arnold down for a nap, and when I get home, I want you in nothing but your heels. I have some ideas floating around in my mind involving chocolate syrup and whipped cream" he finished suggestively.

"You're so nasty" responded Erica with the naughty thoughts already forming inside her

Chapter Two

Kyle & Zoe

"Mr. Swiss, who is the founder of Swiss Pharmaceuticals and a plethora of other major corporations, has just lost a civil suit costing him ten of his most lucrative business beginning with Swiss Pharmaceuticals and ending with Swiss Accounts of America. Mr. Swiss, who is reported to be worth upwards of twenty-five billion dollars, was given a life sentence in the Minnesota department of corrections for his role in the 1996 cold case homicide of Arnold Simmons Sr. For those of you who have been following this case from the beginning, Simmons Sr. was set to win a bidding war for what has been renamed Swiss Pharmaceuticals when Mr. Swiss at the time ordered for him to be executed, which led up to this point today."

The news reporter continued his broadcast as the normally hectic and chaotic conference room of Swiss Accounts sat stunned while listening in on the breaking news report. Fed up, Kyle quickly exited the conference room. Kyle's mind was racing as he pondered on what all of this meant for him. He knew that, with Arnold winning the civil suit, he was nine-out of ten times out of a job. He made it outside of Swiss Accounts with Alu following.

"So, what do you think happens next?" Alu asked as they leaned their backs against the steel structure of Swiss Accounts, while watching traffic. "I don't know what comes next for you, but I'm out of a job" informed Kyle.

"How can you say that?" asked Alu, confused.

Kyle looked over at Alu and began to tell him his history with Arnold for the very first time. He spared him no details, even including the part where Arnold had barged into his condo and shot him over Erica.

"Oh" said Alu once Kyle had finished. "Yeah, you're out of a job, but if you are, so am I" finished Alu, showing his loyalty to Kyle.

Kyle didn't reply right away as his mind went back to the implications of the judge's decision. Financially, he could afford to be laid off. He had more than enough money to last him throughout retirement, but that was the problem, he wasn't ready to retire yet.

"You know, maybe this is all a good sign that it's time for us to step out on our own and form our own firm" announced Kyle.

"Sign and symbols for a conscious mind" replied Alu.

"So, what do you say?"

Alu thought about what Kyle was suggesting and the more he thought, the more it began to make sense. Together, they were already managing twelve of the top fifteen accounts that Swiss

Accounts held and, ever since Mr. Swiss received the life a sentence, several of the clients had requested to end their contracts. It was Alu and Kyle who had convinced them to stay put, now, they could be the same ones to convince them to walk away as they now were.

"I say it sounds like a plan" stated Alu. Again, both men became lost in their own thoughts. Kyle began to fantasize about making their own ambitions come true. He knew what they needed in order to form their practice and knew it wouldn't be hard to find funding. When it came to investors, one person he knew wouldn't hesitate was his best friend, Louis. He also thought about possibly bringing Zoe into the fold.

"Shit!" cursed Kyle aloud. He quickly turned and made his way back inside Swiss Accounts rushing toward the elevator and up to his office. Alu was fast on his heels as he asked Kyle what had happened. "I forgot I'd planned to have dinner with Zoe at home tonight. I was supposed to have been there over an hour ago. She's going to be extremely disappointed" voiced Kyle while running into his office. He grabbed a hold of his blazer and briefcase before rushing towards the exit. He yelled back to Alu "I'm going to draw up a business plan and fax it to you ASAP," and then he was gone.

* * * * *

Kyle pulled up to the home that he and Zoe shared together and killed the engine. He jumped out of his car and ran up to the house.

"I'm going to lose my relationship if I keep this up," he said to himself as he sneaked his way inside. He threw his briefcase aside and called out to Zoe while making his way to the kitchen. After not finding her there, he made his way towards the dining room. He saw that the table was cleared, and that Zoe was nowhere in sight. He made his way into the living room, he found Zoe there balled up on the couch while silently snoring as her dream consumed her. He walked close to her and began to watch her as she slept. She appeared so angelic and peaceful. The sight of her automatically warmed his heart and gave him a feeling of completeness. He bent down close to her ear and began whispering her name softly in an effort to stir her. His efforts worked as she opened her eyes and looked up into his.

"Hey, babe" she greeted sleepily. "When did you make it home?"

"I just got in a few minutes ago" he replied as he sat down on the couch next to her. He took the time to brush the strings of hair from her face before leaning in to lightly peck her on the lips. "I missed you" he relayed.

"I missed you, too" she replied. "Your plate is in the microwave. I tried waiting for you, but after a while, I figured you must've gotten caught up at the office, so I went ahead and ate" she finished as she sat up and leaned her head onto his shoulder. She breathed in his scent and felt

relieved that he was home with her. Ever since they decided to become a couple, Zoe had been living in Chicago with him. Kyle brought his arm around her and brought her closer to him.

"I'm sorry" he told her.

"Sorry for what?" Zoe asked, acting oblivious. "You don't have to keep doing that, you know."

"I know that I can't keep standing you up this way, I know that it affects you despite the fact that you try your hardest not to show it. I don't mean to do it. It's just been very hard for me to separate myself from work lately which is no excuse and that's why I apologize for it."

"Babe, I know that you've been going through a lot at work, I just don't want you to forget that you have a life. I don't want you turning into one of those men that wakes up and goes to sleep inside his office" Zoe stated seriously. She knew how deeply Kyle could consume himself into his work, especially when his stress levels peaked. He had a tendency to try working his problems away.

Kyle looked at Zoe with endearment. He was grateful to have such a considerate woman by his side. He understood that she never wanted to add stress onto him which often kept her from expressing her true feelings to him. He didn't like that fact because he always wanted her to speak her mind to him. "You know that you come before my work and before anything else in my world. I know that I get carried away with work, but those are the times that I need you to stop me and remind me of my priorities" stated Kyle.

"Okay" Zoe replied.

"Okay, what?" asked Kyle as he brought his face into her body playfully.

"Okay, I'll remind you of your priorities" stated Zoe while laughing at Kyle's playfulness as he began to climb all over her. He began planting kisses upon her lips as their playfulness turned into sexual desire. Kyle made his way between Zoe's legs as he began to kiss her. She reciprocated his desire and began undressing him while at the same time he undressed her. Once they were completely naked, Kyle hovered over her with his manhood in hand ready to enter her. She looked up at him seductively while spreading her legs even wider, giving him complete access to her.

"I guess I haven't forgotten all of my priorities" Kyle said right before entering her and gently making love to her.

Chapter Three

Cante & Louis

"What does the word 'love' mean to you?" whispered Louis to Cante as he came up from behind her. He gently placed his hands over her eyes. Leaning back, she pressed her body against his provocatively, sending tingles through both of them. The question posed wasn't one that he expected an answer to. It had become an expression of their relationship. They often referred back to it in order to remind themselves of the commitment they've given to the word 'love'. It was the necessity to always remind one another of how much they meant to each other. It was to remember what love meant for them and to never take what they'd built for granted. They understood that, if they weren't careful, they could easily find themselves neglecting that very word and one another.

Louis slowly removed his hands from Cante's eyes and gently twirled her around so that she could look into his hazel eyes. The compassion that laid within her eyes every time he looked into them always caused his heart to flutter. He had vowed to himself to never turn that look of compassion into one of pain. He was her very first love and knew that the position would determine a lot on her future perspective of the world. He refused to be the one to leave a bitter taste in her mouth when it came to love.

"I have a surprise for you" he stated before grabbing her by the hand, They began trotting through the hot sands back towards their condo as Louis led the way.

"What surprise is that?" asked Cante as she held on tight to his hand.

"If I told you, it wouldn't be a surprise then, would it?" said Louis with a smirk on his face.

Once they made it inside, Louis led Cante to sit down inside the living room before darting off toward their bedroom. He made it over to the dresser and retrieved what he'd come for. Before making his way back to her, he stopped and reviewed his reflection in the full-length mirror. He wanted his appearance to be immaculate as he took the time to smooth his hands over his waves, leaving them perfectly atop his head. Once he was satisfied with his appearance, he said a silent prayer in hopes that she be receptive of his gift. It had taken him some time to decide if he should proceed with giving it to her. His indecisiveness had little to do with him not wanting to, he just wasn't sure how she would respond. He took a moment to open the black velvet box to view the 10-carat platinum and gold engagement ring that he'd purchased for her.

"Marriage" he quietly whispered the word to himself in disbelief.

Was he ready to give one woman all of him for the rest of his existence? He could hardly believe it himself. He had once considered himself one of the biggest playboys to ever grace the earth. Sampler every variety of woman and savoring the moments the flings had lasted. It was fun to him, a freedom that he'd once felt was second to none. Now, he found himself experiencing a different kind of freedom, one that allowed him to fall knowing that in the end there will be one set of arms there to catch him. The time had come for him to make her his wife. She had become everything that he could imagine wanting in a woman. She'd relinquished her past for promiscuity and held on true and faithful to him. She listened to him, took the time to understand him, catered to him, respected him and allowed him to take control of their destiny. Now, he was determined that their destiny was to become one. Slowly, he made his way back to her with his hands held behind his back.

He got closer. "Come on, give it to me" Cante requested eagerly with both hands held out in anticipation. Louis did something she never expected and would remember for the remainder of her life, he got down on one knee.

"Cante" he began. "You have become my sun when it rises in the morning and the stars that shine at night. You have become the breath in my lungs and the blood that's within my veins. I'd never imagined that I could love, let alone love endlessly. You have given me a different perspective on life and how I live it, one without worry, question, or doubt. You have made me happier than I've ever been, and I can no longer picture myself exploring this world without you. That's why I'm here on one knee to ask you to please... do me the honor of being my wife?"

Cante felt as if she was in shock as she watched Louis open the velvet box to allow the carats to glisten before her eyes. A tear slid down her face and her hands shook. She shakily reached out her left hand as Louis removed the ring from the box and put it on her finger.

In a voice filled with glee, surprise, and fulfillment she announced to Louis "Yes, yes I will marry you, Louis Johnson!" then went down to her knees with him and pulled him into her arms.

Louis held her tightly and he felt her shaking as the tears came from her eyes. He had the biggest smile on his face. He was truly happy, happier than he'd ever been in his entire life. This experience helped him to see that material things held little substance. Even with enormous sums of money, vintage vehicles, expensive jewelry and vacation homes scattered all over the world, he would feel incomplete without Cante. He was once a man with an insatiable appetite for women, now the only flavor he desired was Cante.

"I love you so much" he said to Cante as he lifted them to their feet. Next, he gave Alexa the voice command to play Jagged Edge's song, 'Let's Get Married'. The song began booming through the speakers as Cante laid her head against his chest, together they began slowly dancing to their future.

Chapter Four

Alu, Kyle, and Louis

SIX MONTHS LATER

Alu, Louis, and Kyle stood outside the front of Precise Accounts' brand new headquarters, admiring the towering glass and steel edifice. A look of satisfaction was plastered on each of their faces as an overwhelming sense of pride overtook them. The headquarters was built to their satisfaction which gave them hope of similar success for the future. The one hundred twenty story building held offices specializing in almost every area of finance. The primary focus was to provide the service of some of the most highly qualified accountants on the globe. Now their thoughts had become a reality as each man's investment into the business made them equal partners. When Kyle had introduced the idea to Louis in the form of a business plan, Louis was all-in after seeing the profit potential. He had complete faith in his friends' accounting abilities and knew of Alu to be a close second behind Kyle as the most talented accountants around. Factoring in his very own expertise of running corporations, he felt that they couldn't fail.

The investment wasn't much of a risk to him, being it had a minor effect on his nest egg. He knew that in three-to-five years, max, the investment would have paid off itself. Kyle had contributed just as much into the venture which affected his savings. He had several other investments that grossed him a healthy yearly sum. Alu, on the other hand, was in a somewhat different position. He had more riding on the success of this investment than both of his counterparts. His equal part in this caused him to completely deplete his savings account and forced him to take out a loan that would be deemed unfavorable if this investment didn't pay off. He'd taken the risk because he not only had the utmost faith in his own ability to succeed, but he had faith in Kyle's and Louis' abilities. He was determined to work hard because he felt slightly vulnerable knowing of his mortgage payment and other obligations needed to be fulfilled. He couldn't wait to get to work and have the healthy paychecks coming in; the thought alone excited him.

"We did it!" said Alu aloud, interrupting each man's private thoughts.

"I know" replied Kyle before draping his arm over Alu's shoulder.

Louis did the same thing from the other side of Alu before stating, "Now it's time to celebrate our lucrative future with a few bottles of bubbly" stated Louis. "Let's get back inside."

Together, the three men entered back inside the lobby of their establishment. They were welcomed by their entire financial team who were already deeply engrossed into the celebration. All around, hands were being shaken and hugs given as the potential of large profits and paychecks had everyone feeling festive. Kyle walked over to the large buffet table and pulled a bottle of Blair Rose from the metal bucket filled with ice and plenty of champagne. Alu and Louis were right behind him as they both retrieved their own bottles of champagne from the bucket. Separately, they all uncorked their bottles allowing the suds to come spilling from the tops onto the marble flooring below.

"Whew!" Kyle yelled aloud before holding his bottle high into the air.

Alu and Louis both followed suit before Kyle addressed the room, leading them to toast. "To everyone here that's now a part of the financial team of Precise Accounts, I hope that you're ready to take this industry by storm!" The room erupted into applause.

"It is now our opportunity to not only leave our mark on this industry, but to leave our mark on history as well!" Again, the room erupted into applause as Kyle allowed his words to take effect on everyone.

"Now, initially, the journey won't be a walk in the park, considering competition is not only stark, but plentiful. We're now swimming in an ocean filled with sharks, but I have complete faith in the brilliant minds of everyone here and the expertise you possess within your respective fields that not only will we prevail, but that we'll conquer!"

Kyle waited for the cheers to subside before continuing. "We will out-maneuver and force our competition to change their ways of doing business. We will utilize our unique techniques in negotiating, pricing, marketing, advertising, and customer service that will force clients of the competition to reassign to Precise Accounts. I stand here today, in the midst of this great moment in history, with the co-founders of this great venture Mr. Alu Francis and Mr. Louis Johnson and together, we promise you a brighter tomorrow. We promise you professional, respectful, and comfortable work environment. So let us all join together in raising our cups, glasses, and bottles in the air" Kyle paused briefly as everyone in attendance followed him.

"This is to never fearing the unknown, to never being afraid to take advantage of opportunity, to trust, loyalty, friendship, and last but not least, to riches!"

"To riches!" the entire room repeated as they tipped their drinks back and drank to a prosperous future.

Chapter Five

Cante & Louis

Louis pulled up to the curb alongside Ruth Chris' steak house and made his way to Cante's door, opened it and allowed her to exit. He opened the back door and held his hand out to Big Momma, helping her out of the car. Big Momma locked her arm with Louis's on his left side as Cante followed suit and did the same to his right. Together, the three of them made their way inside of the restaurant. As they entered, the smell of steaks grilling wafted past their noses, causing their stomachs to growl. They were greeted at the door by the hosts who led them to their table.

Once everyone was situated, Big Momma began to speak. "Chilli, you have me dressed up all nicely and sitting in this high-class restaurant and I don't even know what we're celebrating" complained Big Momma to Louis.

"You'll find out soon enough" assured Louis with Cante by his side.

"I hope so, because I sure don't like surprises. Besides that, I don't like eating any food that I haven't personally prepared myself" nagged Big Momma before picking the menu up and examining it. "Chilli, do you see the price of the food in here? For these prices I could've fed you for a month straight" she announced astounded.

Cante couldn't help but to chuckle from Big Momma's reaction. She admired the way Big Momma always said what came to her mind, no matter if it was obnoxious or not.

"Don't worry yourself about the price, Big Momma. I know you're not into surprises, but I believe that this will be one surprise you enjoy." The waitress made her way over to collect their orders, Big Momma and Cante allowed Louis to order for them. After patiently waiting for almost twenty minutes and making frivolous conversation, their food was brought out to them along with a bottle of champagne for Cante and Louis and a cranberry juice for Big Momma. Together, the trio enjoyed their meal mostly in silence. After the main courses was finished and the dessert had been devoured, their conversation resumed.

"Okay, Big Momma, I know you've been wondering why we've brought you out tonight and the reason is because we have something very important to share with you" relayed Louis.

"Okay, Chilli, I've waited long enough, what is it?"

Louis looked toward Cante with admiration in his eyes as she looked at him with the same affection. "Do you want to tell her, or would you like me to?" Louis asked Cante.

"If you want me to tell her, I would, but if you want to, then go ahead" Cante replied.

"It's up to you" Louis stated.

"Would one of you just go ahead and tell me, I can't take the suspense any longer" voiced

Big Momma impatient.

"Okay, okay" Louis said while chuckling to himself at Big Momma's lack of patience.

"Well, the reason why we brought you out tonight is because we wanted you to celebrate with us this important chapter of our lives that we've come upon and that is that we're getting married!"

"Oh my God, Chilli!" shouted Big Momma much louder than she'd intended. She looked from Louis over to Cante just as Cante lifted her left hand so that Big Momma could see the massive engagement ring on her finger. Big Momma covered her mouth in shock as tears began to fall from her eyes.

"Big Momma" said Louis as he got up and made his way around to her side of the table. This was his very first time witnessing Big Momma shed a tear. Big Momma wrapped him inside her arms once he made it over to her and continued crying, he hugged her back.

"Big Momma, are you okay?" asked Cante from the other side of the table.

Big Momma separated herself from Louis before she began to speak. "Never mind me, Chilli," she replied while using a napkin to wipe away her tears. "These tears here are tears of joy. Chilli, I'm so happy for both of you. It warms my heart to see how far along he has come. I once thought that I'd never get the chance to see this day" finished Big Momma as the tears continued to fall from her eyes.

Louis placed his arm around Big Momma in a comforting manner. "Well, Big Momma, you're here to see the day" he stated proudly.

Big Momma gathered her composure. "I remember when my husband had first proposed to me. It was 1957, and I was just seventeen years of age. That day was the happiest day of my life. We were both young and very much in love, but a lot of people didn't agree with it, stating that we were too young to make such a life-long commitment. They said it, but neither one of us heard it. We were young, but we weren't naive to the fact that we had a long, challenging road ahead of ourselves. The beauty of it was that we embraced those possibilities, we also had embraced the fact that we had some amazing times ahead of ourselves as well. You see, that's the thing about marriage, it isn't meant to be perfect. Marriage is a journey of both ups and downs. It is a joint effort that requires communication, understanding, sacrifice, commitment, desire, and the perseverance to endure whatever comes your way. It's those who choose to only embrace the wonderful moments that won't last. It's those who can't stand the rain, but chase after every rainbow that won't last. It's those that live in the fairy tale vision that the movies portray of marriage that won't last. I can remember a time in my marriage that me and my husband couldn't even stand to sleep in the same room. We were twenty years into marriage and the spark just wasn't there like it once was; but the love still remained. Love is what got us through; well, that along with prayer. We not only had faith in love, but we had faith in God as well, and the two are both indestructible powers. As long as you don't forget how to love one another, then you'll be able to last. We remembered what love meant to us both and, even though it took three years for us to

share a room again, we eventually did. We needed that three years to help us remember. We needed that time apart to miss one another's touch, presence, and desire. Even though I didn't miss that loud snoring of his" Big Momma said more of an afterthought as she chuckled to herself.

"What I'm telling you is that marriage is a commitment that comes with a lot of obstacles. It's the commitment to one another, it's the love for one another. It's the willingness to fight for one another and never leave your partner to fight alone that you must have. You can't allow television, social media, or society to dictate your vision of what you've developed. Make up your minds together and work with each other to be as one and to remain as one."

Big Momma paused briefly to remove Louis' arm from around her neck. "Now, get back on over there, Chilli with that lovely future wife of yours."

Louis got up and made his way around the table, once there, he hugged and kissed Cante gently as Big Momma looked on with a lovely smile on her face.

Chapter Six

Kyle & Zoe

Kyle stood inside of his office looking out of the massive window that overlooked the busy streets of Chicago. He was lost in thought about the next move in order to get Precise Accounts in the position to lead all their competitor's. They were doing pretty good to start, locking up major long-term contracts with some well-established corporations. Business was better than he'd initially expected; but still, he desired better. He'd been hearing of moves that Arnold and Simmons Accounts were making in order to try cornering the market and he refused to allow them to do so. He'd underestimated Arnold and his savviness to do business, but the more he sat down with potential clients, the more they used the possibility of signing with Simmons Accounts as a bargaining tool. He'd lost a few potential clients in negotiation and witnessed them take their business over to Simmons Accounts, which showed Kyle that Arnold was a force to be reckoned with. This is what currently held Kyle in limbo, forcing him to have to think up new and creative techniques to lock clients in.

He began to think about the most recent promotional scheme that his advertising director had presented to him when he heard his office door open then close. Assuming that it was Susan his receptionist, he announced that he didn't wish to be disturbed. His thoughts went back to the promotional scheme and the budget that he'd approved to go alone with it. He felt that if it all was to get put together correctly, then it would achieve excellent results. He began to think about Arnold again and how difficult he was making things. He had become a challenge, but to Kyle, a challenge was a motivating factor. Again, his thoughts were interrupted as he felt a hand gently placed upon his shoulder.

"Susan, I thought I said that I didn't wish to be bothered" he stated before turning on his heels to face her. He was taken by surprise once he realized that the person in his office wasn't Susan, but Zoe.

"I sent Susan home for the day" Zoe stated before placing a plate of food on the desk opposite from them. She stood before him with her blond hair pulled back into a tight ponytail just the way she knew Kyle liked. Her pouty lips were bright with red lipstick and the beige coat that she wore stopped just above her matching Christian Dior red bottom heels. Before Kyle could reply, Zoe began to unfasten her trench coat. Slowly it opened, revealing her naked frame. She discarded the coat completely as her plumped, snow white breasts sat up perfectly before him. Her light-pink nipples stood at attention from her excitement as Kyle glanced down at her neatly trimmed pubic area, which caused his manhood to stiffen. He glanced over her long legs before bringing his eyes back up to look into her emerald green ones. He could tell by the seductive look in her eyes that she knew she had him exactly where she wanted him.

"I figured you wouldn't mind" she stated regarding her dismissal of Susan. She took a couple of steps backward right before resting her bare ass on the edge of the desk and opening her legs up. She batted her eyes seductively before tilting her head back and allowing her hands to roam all over her body in the most hypnotizing way. She moaned softly. "I wanted it to be just the two of us." Kyle began to take slow and deliberate steps toward her. He was extremely aroused. The show that she was putting on for him made the bulge in his slacks stick out several inches.

He made it over to her, leaning in and kissing her passionately about the lips. She wrapped her legs around him as she reciprocated his desire, kissing him with extreme passion. Kyle separated his lips from hers, causing a small gasp to escape her mouth.

He began trailing his kisses down her neck, collar bone and down her breasts. He took his time, gently nibbling and sucking on her hardened nipples, giving them the special attention that she loved. She leaned back, poking her chest out even more so that Kyle could devour her breasts completely. She began to moan aloud just as her juices began to drip down her legs.

Slowly, Kyle began to trail his kisses down and over her stomach. He placed soft and gentle kisses over her skin, taking his time as he made it down to her glistening sex. He placed soft kisses upon her moist labia, before bringing his hands up and using his thumbs to gently spread them, softly kissing her insides. The feeling of his full lips upon her caused her to gasp continuously and her legs to shake uncontrollably. He began to lick her in perfect circles, going from one side to the next while occasionally sticking his tongue deep inside her. She brought her hand down and onto his head, pushing him into her even more. He moved his right thumb up and began rubbing it against her clit, the unexpected change caused her to orgasm. The taste of her cum excited him as he began to gently bite and nibble on her with renewed determination. The pleasure was so intense that it caused Zoe to scoot backward on the desktop to try escaping it.

Kyle placed a hand on either side of her thighs locking her into place as his tongue lashed out like a snake, sending her into a frenzy of moans, gasping and panting just as another orgasm approached. Kyle sensed this and held her even tighter, applying more pressure with his tongue. He quickly took his tongue from her labia and brought it to her clit, flicking it gently. The feeling took Zoe over the edge for a second time, sending her fluids flowing out like a river. Kyle lapped it all up before making it to his feet. He watched as Zoe lay panting and quietly gasping.

He began to unbuckle his slacks, he pulled them down and stepped out of them before doing the same thing with his boxers. Zoe regained her strength as she sat up atop his desk. Kyle stepped back into her as they embraced and kissed one another frantically. Zoe undid his tie and eagerly ripped his shirt open, sending several buttons flying across the room. She got him out of his shirt as they continued their tongue kiss. She rubbed her hand over his muscular chest and abs.

Next, she reached and grabbed a hold of his length, stroking it up and down. He felt hot within her hands as she tried to guide him inside her. Kyle lifted her leg slightly before penetrating her, sliding deep inside her. Zoe moaned out his name as he filled her up. He began to stroke in and out of her while looking deeply into her eyes. Her facial expressions began to turn him on even more, causing him to quickly pick up his pace. She wrapped her legs around his waist and her arms around his neck as he picked her up and carried her over to the massive window that overlooked the city. Leaning her body against it, he began to grind himself in and out of her, causing her to scratch whatever part of him her hands could touch. He held her there for several minutes before carrying her back over to his desk. Letting her down he quickly turned her around. He took her left leg and propped it up onto his desk. Zoe moaned as she looked at him over her shoulder. He guided himself back into her while gripping her hips. He began to slowly bring her back into him, causing the sound of their bodies slapping against one another to fill his room. Zoe began whipping her head from side to side, losing herself in his stroke. "Damn" said Kyle, as he felt himself on the verge of exploding.

He removed his hand from her hip and reached out to grab a hold of her ponytail. He tilted her head slightly to the side so that they could look into one another's eyes as he picked up his pace, grunting loudly as she moaned even louder. He went deep inside of her one more time before exploding. The euphoric feeling caused him to shake before he collapsed his body onto hers as they lay flat against the desktop. Panting loudly, they began kissing one another for several seconds as Kyle slipped from within her womb. Slowly, he stood up, allowing her to as well. He began to get dressed as she slipped her trench coat back on before walking up to him, she stood on her tippy toes and kissed him once more.

"Since you are having a hard time making it home, I figured I'd bring home to you" she paused briefly as she retrieved his plate filled with food from the other side of the desk and handed it to him. "You may get back to work now" she finished before turning on her heels and walking out of his office leaving him standing there with a satisfied smirk on his face.

Chapter Seven

Arnold & Erica

Arnold was in full force with his reconstruction of Swiss Accounts. The first thing he did was to switch the name from Swiss to Simmons in memory of his late father. The next thing he did was fire most of the old staff and hire new people. He really didn't have much to do in the firing phase, being that most of the previous staff had already resigned. He'd anticipated this occurrence ahead of time because he knew that most the staff was loyal to one another, being that they'd worked in unison for years.

He'd heard through the grapevine that Kyle had formed his own accounting firm with Alu and Louis as equal partners. Most of the previous staff at Swiss Accounts now maintained employment there. Arnold took to recruiting several young, brilliant accountants from all over the world. He also recruited several marketing directors, public relation specialists, customer service directors, and advertising specialists to help in forming a powerful team. Arnold was feeling optimistic about the direction that Simmons Accounts was headed in and witnessed the progress through the numerous amounts of wealthy clients that occupied their ledger.

Arnold had become obsessed with the progression of Simmons Accounts and most of his time was now being consumed there. He felt far from where he wanted them to be and the fact that Precise Accounts was pulling in more clients and revenue than his firm had begun to eat at his ego. He sat down at his office desk and booted up his laptop in preparation of doing a little competitive analysis. He began by looking into Kyle's business associates Louis Johnson and Alu Francis. He looked into Louis and noted that he'd recently been named by Forbes as one of the fastest rising billionaires. He researched several of Louis' corporations, all were well-known blue-chip stocks offered by Dow and the S&P 500 and all were very successful and lucrative; this really impressed him. He went into Louis' past and noted that he'd attended Illinois University along with Kyle and had also graduated with Latin Honors, Magna Cum Laude.

As he continued looking, he couldn't seem to find a flaw within Louis and concluded that he was a loyal ally of Kyle. Next, he typed in the name of Alu Francis and watched as information popped up. The Arabian accountant graduated from Stanford University valedictorian with several honors. He began to look into Alu's investment history and noted that this was his very first time stepping out as an entrepreneur. He probed more into Alu's past, noting that he was originally from Saudi Arabia and had migrated to the States with his parents when he was only five years of age. Alu's upbringing was modest, and he'd really just come into fortune with the acquisition of the World National Bank account when he was still employed through Swiss Accounts. Arnold realized that Alu was taking extreme risk by stepping out with Kyle and Louis to form Precise Accounts. Most of his net worth was tied into the investment.

"Uhm..." said Arnold to himself. "If that isn't trust and loyalty then I don't know what is."

Not being able to find any flaws within Alu and Louis, he decided to look into Precise Accounts' financial records. He noted that they were reporting net-gains since their forming and was compliant with all of the Internal Revenue Service and Securities and Exchange Commission's regulations. After not finding any loose links in the chain, he decided to shut down his computer. He leaned back into his dark brown massive leather chair and interlocked his fingers behind his head. He needed an angel; something that would give him a competitive advantage and help to bring Precise Accounts to its demise. His mind began to wonder and the thoughts that surfaced were devious to say the least. He'd have to get creative. Maybe he would have to grease a couple of palms; throw a little money around to create some dirt or corruption. His mind continued wandering. "There's a crack in every floor, you just have to find it."

Kyle's team appeared to be running a tight ship, but he knew that things weren't always what they seemed. Ego and greed, he understood was most men's downfall. He was determined to find their weakness; this was the art of war and he would use every weapon within his arsenal to win. Just then, a plan began to formulate inside of his mind. "Divide and conquer" he said to himself before reaching for his office phone. A smile crept over his face as he dialed a number and waited for the party on the other end to answer.

Chapter Eight

Arnold & Erica

Erica sat with her parents at a restaurant in downtown Minneapolis dining around a soft tone of jazz. Erica and Arnold had invited her parents out as they did weekly to try enjoying their company while seeking guidance and advice about life and marriage. As Erica and her parents awaited Arnold's arrival, they sat eating and chatting.

"How are you enjoying the new house so far?" Asked Mr. Caldwell of the home that Arnold had recently purchased at Erica's request.

"I'm loving it, Poppa! It's very spacious, the ceilings are extremely high, the kitchen is mostly marble with several preparation areas and I love the fact that there's nothing but hardwood flooring around the rest of the house. I was getting so tired of baby Arnold ruining the carpet."

"How has the decorating been coming along?" inquired Mrs. Caldwell.

"It's actually going well. It's very exciting to make my visions reality. I feel so much like a kid that's playing dress up, but instead, I'm dressing up my home. The only difficult part is the designers don't have an item I've picked out in stock. Most times, I have to wait several weeks before they do" complained Erica.

"Well, honey, when you want something done right and you're meticulous about it, you have to have patience in order to see it materialize."

"Yeah, you know how meticulous I could be at times and that's partly the reason why most of the rooms are still without paint or furniture." Erica continued.

"You should lower your standards just a little sweetie," advised Mrs. Caldwell.

"No, you shouldn't" interrupted Mr. Caldwell. "The moment that you begin to lower your standards in others, you stray. Always seek what you deserve no matter what."

"I understand." replied Erica before looking down at her watch. She noted that Arnold was almost two hours late and began to wonder if he even make it. Her father must've read her mind as he stated. "He probably got caught up in a meeting, he's probably rushing here as we speak."

"I hope so. He seems to be getting caught up in meetings more often than I care to mention" complained Erica.

"That's what comes along with running major companies. A hard-working and ambitious man is a strong man" stated Mrs. Caldwell.

"And a lonely woman is a vulnerable one" replied Erica.

The table became quiet after Erica's last comment. Mrs. Caldwell looked over at Mr. Caldwell as she tried to digest what Erica had just said. Erica realized that her last statement hadn't come out the way she'd intended it to.

"Not that kind of vulnerable" she explained.

"What you're saying is that his not being home is beginning to have a negative effect on you?" asked Mr. Caldwell. Erica simply shook her head in confirmation. "If I recall correctly, you told me that you'd encouraged him to proceed with handling these ventures in the way that he needed."

"Yes, I did, but I didn't know that it would consume as much of his time that it has. I mean, I support him and all I just wish he would find more time to be home with me and his child" responded Erica.

"Have you voiced this to him?" asked Mrs. Caldwell.

"I feel like I shouldn't have to"

"Why shouldn't you?" asked Mr. Caldwell.

"Because he knows how much I hate to appear inconsiderate and selfish" said Erica.

"Selfish is you expecting him to know something that you haven't yet voiced. Especially when it contradicts your original view. It's selfish to expect him to fix something that he doesn't know is broken. Think about him as you want him to think about you." advised Mrs. Caldwell.

"But it should be self-explanatory that we want you home at least a few days out of the week. It's like he doesn't even recognize that we miss him and need him home. We've been lucky to see him twice a month. It's becoming difficult having to explain to our son why his father is barely home" Erica went on.

"Honey, you have to understand that he'd just had a lot of responsibility dropped on him all of a sudden. Don't you think you're being inconsiderate to the circumstances?" stated Mr. Caldwell.

"I didn't ask for any of this" complained Erica.

"And neither did he" announced Mrs. Caldwell.

Erica shot her mom a look that said *whose side are you on?*

"I'm just stating the obvious" stated Mrs. Caldwell.

"Baby, neither of you asked for this. This all was thrown on you just like the loss of his father was thrown on him," informed Mr. Caldwell.

"Father, please don't use that to excuse him" Erica complained.

"It's a factual statement whether you want to admit it or not. I'm just saying that this has all been a lot for him just as well as it's been for you. Maybe he's using his workload as an escape from the reality that his father is no longer here" he said.

"His wife and child should be his escape," stated Erica stubbornly.

Again, the table became quiet. Mr. Caldwell gave Mrs. Caldwell a look that said *please talk to her.* This situation wasn't an unfamiliar one for them. Mrs. Caldwell once had similar complaints many years ago.

"First off, you have to know that he loves you as well as baby Arnold. But you have to allow things to run their course and understand that people often cope in different ways." counseled Mrs. Caldwell.

"So, how am I supposed to cope with basically raising a child alone because my husband is barely home enough to help me?" asked Erica.

"I'm sure that it's only temporary" assured Mr. Caldwell.

"Okay, but that doesn't take away from the fact that it's my current reality" finished Erica.

Mr. Caldwell looked down at his watch before glancing toward the door of the restaurant. When his eyes made it back over to Erica's he recognized the pain and frustration that was in them. He understood what she was going through, but he also understood the position that Arnold was in. It was a time when Erica was a child and too young to notice that he was barely home. Mrs. Caldwell had felt the same way as Erica. However, he was the provider for their home and felt it necessary to do what he needed. He'd gotten Mrs. Caldwell to understand that it wasn't that he didn't want to be home, but that he had to make this sacrifice in order to provide them a better future.

"Some things take a little more time to fall into place, darling, you can't put pressure on him or rush things. Patience is a virtue" advised Mrs. Caldwell.

Erica knew that what her parents were telling her was the truth. She just wanted her husband home more to show her and their son the attention they needed. She knew that she was being slightly selfish by not allowing Arnold the time he needed to find that balance, to satisfy his work obligation as well as his family obligations.

"Have faith, baby" comforted Mr. Caldwell.

"Okay, Poppa."

The three of them sat talking for a couple of hours more with Erica constantly glancing down at her watch and over toward the door of the restaurant. Mr. Caldwell tried keeping her mind off the fact that Arnold hadn't shown. He felt bad but knew that Arnold was just trying to do what a man is supposed to do.

Once he'd come convinced that Arnold wouldn't show, he stood up.

"Come on ladies, let's get out of here" said to his wife and daughter before he led them out of the restaurant.

Chapter Nine

Cante & Louis

Cante sat in the comfort of her living room in her boy shorts and t-shirt while listening to Monica's "Why I Love You So Much" and going over a few pamphlets with possible wedding destinations. She was in a state of bliss thinking about her upcoming wedding to Louis. She couldn't believe that they'd made it to this point in their relationship. What started off as just a night of fun, ended in a future lifetime commitment. She'd never believed that she would marry, she couldn't picture something so routine appealing to her. She'd always viewed marriage as more of a business commitment or obligation. She believed people only really got married for a couple of reasons, one being because of religious pressures and the other because of society's pressures when a baby comes into play.

To her, these two possibilities were the only reasons, why else would someone commit to something so treacherous? Now, here she was, planning to get married and feeling ecstatic about it. This situation is what gave her a third outlook on why two people would get married; because they felt like they couldn't live without one another. She smiled to herself at the thought because that's exactly how she felt pertaining to Louis. She could no longer imagine her existence separate from him. She knew that he felt the same way about her. He'd changed so much since the day they'd met. He did everything in his power to continuously make her feel secure, special, desired, and loved. She respected the fact that he never tried hiding his emotions from her. He never feigned too much bravado to openly show her his love and affection. Every time she thought about this once impossible man securely giving her the key to his heart, it brought a tingle in between her legs, and now was no different.

"So, this how you feel?" asked Louis of the song Cante had playing as he walked inside of the living room toward her.

"You make me feel this way." responded Cante. Louis made his way to sit down beside her on the leather couch. Cante sat the pamphlets down before staring into Louis' eyes. "Tell me about it" said Louis.

Cante smiled. "Let me see, where should I begin?" she said as she sat her hand onto his lap. "I'm just thinking about how hard I've fallen in love with you. I had once told myself monogamy was for people who needed someone to validate their existence. I felt it was for people who couldn't stand to be alone and didn't have the heart to explore the world as such. Now that I've met you, it's hard for me to understand how I could've lived life so long alone. Now, I can't imagine sharing my life with no one but you. I can't imagine another man if that man isn't you. You did something to me that words alone can't explain, and I love it. I love everything about it, Louis. I truly believe with all of my heart that my existence goes hand-in-hand with yours and I wouldn't have it any other way." finished Cante.

Louis leaned in and began to kiss Cante passionately just as the song changed to Brian McKnight's "Love of My Life". Louis sat his hands on Cante's thigh and allowed them to travel upwards as the kiss turned heated. Cante gasped into Louis' mouth as he slipped his tongue into hers. He let his hand travel up her love box slowly rubbing the material that shielded it. Cante opened her legs a little wider as she leaned back against the arm of the couch. She broke away from their kiss and laid her head back toward the ceiling as her eyes closed. Louis began to kiss her neck as he climbed between her legs. He allowed his kiss to trail down her collar bone as he firmly grinded himself into her, allowing his friction to heat her up even more.

Cante began reaching out to remove his shirt; he allowed it to come off before doing the same to her leaving her with her bra and boy shorts on. He reached behind to unclamp her bra before removing it as well causing her perky breasts to giggle slightly. She reached to pull at his pajama pants, which he helped her remove. Stepping out of them, he stood before her with his manhood standing at attention. She licked her lips at the sight, while slightly lifting her ass from the couch and scooting out of her boy shorts. She sat up on the couch and reached to wrap Louis' throbbing member inside her hand. She stroked it several times while looking up into his eyes. Louis looked down at her and felt himself growing an extra inch from her touch. Slowly, she leaned in and gently kissed the head of his manhood. He gasped and leaned his head back from the euphoric feeling. Next, she allowed her tongue to swirl around before taking him fully into her mouth. Louis began to moan from his fiance giving him extreme pleasure, she sucked him for a few minutes before he felt himself on the verge of coming. He pulled back to save himself before getting down to his knees. He lifted both Cante's legs to the air before allowing them to rest on his shoulders.

Cante allowed her hand to roam the top of his head as they looked at one another deeply in the eyes. She brought her hands to the back of his head and pulled him towards her sex as she leaned into the cushions with her eyes closed. Louis brought his lips down and gently placed a kiss on Cante's pussy. She gasped from the feeling as his tongue shacked out of his mouth and into the crease, parting it as he darted his tongue in and out of her. He did it several times, causing her to moan consistently. He then began to gently flick her clit, which he knew had the power to send her over the edge. He flicked slowly at first, then faster and faster as her moans told him that she was right where he wanted her to be. Her legs began to shake, and her juices began to flow, filling his tongue with a delectable taste. He licked her for several minutes before he let her legs down from his shoulders. He allowed them to fall into his muscular arms, bending them slightly as he stood between her legs. She lifted herself slightly as she reached out and grabbed a hold of his pulsating dick. She rubbed it up and down guiding him into her. She gasped loudly as her head snapped backwards. Louis slowly leaned in, going deeper within her. She reached up and wrapped her arms around his neck bringing him to her as their tongues darted back and forth. Louis began stroking in and out of her, occasionally laying inside of her to the hilt before pulling out and repeating the motion. Cante wrapped her legs around his back, giving him full access to her. He placed his hands firmly on the seating of the couch and began to speed up, working his hips in a circular motion while doing so.

"Louis…" Cante moaned his name aloud; she felt herself on the verge of cumming again as he hit the tender spots that were deep within her. Louis picked up this pace even more as the sounds of their skins contacting began to make its own music throughout. "Fuck, Cante," Louis moaned as he felt himself on the verge.

"Cum inside me, Louis, make me cum, I want to feel it," moaned Cante as she could no longer control herself. Louis released deep within her confines as she came simultaneously, her walls contracting and gripping his manhood. As their orgasms subsided, Louis laid his body into Cante's, exhausted.

Cante kissed his neck several times as she whispered "I love you, Louis." Louis enjoyed the feel of her lips on his neck. "I love you too, Cante, the love of my life."

Chapter Ten

Kyle & Zoe

"So, tell me, what is the objective of this game?" Kyle asked the carny.

"The goal is to get as many of these gold rings to land around the little pole there as you could. You get Five Rings, if you get all five then you get to pick one of the large prizes. If you get four, you can pick from one of the medium prizes, if you get three you can choose a small prize, anything less than three, you get to walk away with a good try." finished the carny to Kyle, just as Zoe latched onto Kyle's arm.

"Okay," replied Kyle to the carny as he rolled up his sleeves.

"Babe, you have to get all five because I want one of the large stuffed animals" stated Zoe.

"Baby said she wants one of the large stuffed animals so one of the large stuffed animals she shall get" finished Kyle with a determined look in his eyes. The carny handed Kyle the five rings. "Let the games begin." Zoe took a step back to give Kyle his space.

"You got this, babe" she encouraged him as he went into action, he tossed the first ring in the air which landed perfectly on the pole. He tossed the second one and got the same result.

"Let's go, babe" cheered Zoe as Kyle tossed the third ring and got it to land as the first two had. He was on the fourth ring and was determined not to let Zoe down. He tossed it in the air, and it landed on the pole without a problem. "Okay, babe, you only gotta get one more. If you win this prize for me, I'll give you a special prize when we make it home tonight" said Zoe suggestively.

The carny caught the hint. "No pressure, but it sounds like a lot is riding on this last ring, don't screw up, bud."

"I got this" replied Kyle before licking his lips and unwinding his shoulders. He got himself into the perfect stance and prepared to make the final toss. Concentrating, he slung his arm back and let it go. "Fuck" cursed Kyle aloud as the ring came out of his hand awkwardly.

He watched as it flipped several times while in the air before finally making it to the pole. It hit the pole and made a loud *ding* sound before propelling back into the sky. Zoe watched it in anticipation as the ring appeared to stall mid-air before coming back down and landing directly on the pole.

"Yes!! Yes! Babe, you did it!" screamed Zoe, hugging Kyle around the neck.

"I told you, what the Queen wants, she shall get" joked Kyle before giving the carny a wink.

"We have a winner!" stated the carny. "You have the choice of any large stuffed animal above" he informed them.

"I want the panda" stated Zoe excitedly.

"Okay" replied the carny as he extracted the panda from the wire it was attached to before handing it to Zoe. "Why the panda, I thought the tiger was your favorite animal?" asked Kyle.

"It is, but I just love the color of the panda" replied Zoe.

"The panda is just black and white" stated Kyle confused.

"Which I believe is the perfect mix" replied Zoe before licking her lips and giving Kyle a seductive look.

"Enough said" responded Kyle.

They continued to walk as Zoe held the stuffed animal close to her body. Kyle reached over and tapped Zoe's ass before pulling her into him. They walked past several other couples who seemed to be enjoying one another just as much as the two of them were. It was the Fourth of July and Zoe and Kyle were celebrating at the state carnival. They played just about every game and rode almost every ride, enjoying themselves like two children. It was getting late, and the firework display was going to be taking place.

"I think we should head back over towards our tent; I believe the fireworks should be starting soon" stated Kyle.

"I'm so excited to watch the fireworks; the display seems to get better every year" responded Zoe full of glee.

"Yeah, I'm super excited as well. I think this year's display will be one year we will remember for the rest of our lives."

As they made it back to their tent, Kyle felt the butterflies begin to swarm inside his stomach. He'd been waiting for this moment the entire day. Together, they stood outside of their tent just as all the displays were preparing to take off. Zoe leaned her body into Kyle's as he wrapped his arms around her from the back.

"I really wish Big Momma could have come along with us," said Zoe almost sadly. "I tried to convince her, but she refused because she throws her own display every year for the children in the neighborhood." informed Kyle.

"I should have expected something like that from Big Momma, she's such a godsend" said Zoe in admiration.

"That's what I've been trying to say since I was a kid."

"Babe, it's been three years since I've met your Big Momma and you still haven't taken the trip with me to meet my parents" complained Zoe.

"It's not like I've been avoiding it. Every time we set a date, our schedules end up conflicting, but set up another date and I promise to you I won't let anything get in the way this time."

"Promise?"

"Scout's honor" finished Kyle as he thought to himself that meeting her parents would be necessary after the night. Just then they watched as the first firework was sent up the light the night sky.

"Here we go," stated Zoe excitedly.

The crowd began to "OH" and "AH" as more and more fireworks began to light up the sky. Zoe snuggled her body even closer into Kyle's as she embraced the moment. Kyle unwrapped one of his hands from Zoe's body and discreetly reached inside of his pocket. He felt the velvet material against the palm of his hand before removing the box from his pocket. He released Zoe completely and took a step back then in front of her, obstructing her view of the fireworks.

"What are you doing, babe? You're making us miss the display "complained Zoe.

Kyle looked Zoe deep into the eyes right before he went down to one knee.

"Zoe, the moment that I laid eyes on you, I knew that you were someone special. As time went on, you showed me that I was correct. You've loved me consistently even when I was afraid and held doubts. You never abandoned me even though over the years I've given you plenty of reasons to. You've given me the strength and the courage to be confident, to be unafraid and to believe in true love again. I feel like God has caused our paths to cross the way he did for a reason and I look to one day stand before God and vow to him to be the man for you that he created me to be forever. So, Zoe Fields would you please marry me?"

Zoe held her hand over her mouth as she looked onto Kyle in disbelief. She felt her tears begin to well up as her emotions took hold. She'd been waiting for this day to happen again ever since the passing of her late husband. She'd been waiting to one day be the wife to a man that she always pictured herself being. She'd overcome her flaws and became a stronger woman, now she felt like God was blessing her with another opportunity at happiness.

"Yes! Yes! Kyle I will marry you" replied Zoe as Kyle gently grabbed a hold of her hand and slipped the seven-carat diamond ring onto her finger.

Zoe wiped a tear away as Kyle rose and they looked into one another's eyes before they began to passionately kiss as the fireworks lit up the night's sky around them.

Part 5

"He came along unexpectedly, catching my heart off-guard and overwhelming it with extreme pleasure. It was his unexpected appearance that caused my soul to soar, disregard the negative possibilities, and false folklore. It is him that runs my mind rampant with thoughts of the future and extreme bliss. It is him, who has made me confident and strong even though I get weak from his tender kiss. It is him, who has loved me through and through. Now it is him that I will proudly give my vows to!"

-Zoe Fields

Chapter Eleven

The inside of Precise Accounts headquarters was deafly quiet and dark seeing that everyone that was employed there had ended their shifts several hours earlier so that they could make it home to their families. The only sound coming from within the building was from a lone set of footsteps of a cautious creeper. The footsteps were almost silent as the intruder carefully approached the door that he was seeking. He removed his lock picking kit from the napsack that was thrown over his back. He began to slowly go to work on the lock, it took only seconds before he jimmied it and heard it click. He quietly turned the knob and felt a sense of relief when the door pushed open. He closed the door behind himself and made his way over to the massive oakwood desk that sat at the center of the office with a computer sitting neatly atop it. He knew what he'd come for and he began rummaging through the drawers of the desk in search of it. It took him several minutes before he came across the manila folder that held very classified material. He stuffed the folder inside his napsack before again throwing the pouch back over his shoulders.

He quickly began to boot up the computer, pecking at the keys as he hacked the pass codes. Once he cracked the code, he watched with a smile as the computer lit up. He clicked on several sensitive links, taking his time to meticulously change dates, times, names, and other pertinent information. His smile spread as he falsified the final report before shutting down the computer and completing his task. Instantly, he froze in place, he sat really still and concentrated as he could've sworn he'd heard movement coming from outside of the office. The sound caused him to jump to his feet and scramble over toward the massive leather couch that sat off to the side of the room, using it to conceal himself just as the office door was pushed open.

* * * * *

"I could've sworn I locked up when I ended the day earlier" Kyle said into his phone concerning his unlocked office door.

He walked inside his office and made it over to his desk. "No, baby, I am not getting old, and my memory isn't fading. Yeah, no, Susan doesn't enter my office when I'm out. Okay, but back to what we was talking about…. So, which part of your body did you say you wanted me to start off licking first?" Kyle before he plopped down into his swivel chair allowing it to rock back and forth from side to side as he smirked to himself while listening to Zoe's reply.

"Damn, you not playing, you want me to get straight down to business huh?" Kyle replied before opening his desk drawer in search of the file he'd come to retrieve.

He searched through the drawer and quickly came across the file before removing it and sitting it on top of his desk.

"Uhm, I see you're feeling feisty. I'm saying I'll do that, but once I'm done, you have to do that lil thing that you know I like" stated Kyle through his phone as he trapped it between his ear and shoulder and leaned back inside his chair and interlaced his fingers behind his head. He was really enjoying the conversation and found that it was brightening his mood from his earlier irritation of having to run into the office at such a late hour. He continued to listen while Zoe enticed him with phone sex. He felt his loins stir from the suggestions that Zoe was whispering through the phone.

"Hold on real quick, baby" said Kyle suddenly through the phone as he sat up straight and began to listen attentively to his surroundings. He sat still and tried to make sure that he'd heard a sound coming from within his office. He silently sat his phone atop of his desk and slowly reached inside of his desk drawer to retrieve the Glock .9mm that he kept there for emergencies. He stood as he inserted a hollow tip into the chamber. He kept his gaze firmly at the area of the sound, refusing to miss a thing. He aimed his forearm in that direction and began to take slow, deliberate steps toward the sound. He carefully crept up on the couch in a crouching stance while still aiming the Glock. As he came upon the couch, he took a second to pause as he readied himself just before he swiftly swirled around the couch with his Glock locked and loaded.

"Goddamnit!" Kyle cursed aloud at himself once he realized that no one was there. His heartbeat rapidly as the excitement was still fresh. Relief began to wash over him, and he laughed at himself from his paranoia. He put the gun down and let it rest at his side, clicking on the safety as he made his way back over to his desk. He picked up his phone before placing the firearm back inside the confines of his desk.

"Yeah, I'm here. No, everything's fine. I just thought I'd heard something" voiced Kyle before he retrieved his file from atop his desk and made his way to exit his office.

"Yeah, I know, but it's better to be safe than sorry…" He finished as he opened his office door to leave. Before exiting, he quickly peered back over his shoulder, then he laughed at himself once again from being paranoid as he closed and locked his office door.

* * * * *

It took several minutes after Kyle had left before the intruder moved a muscle. He silently cursed himself for the bold move he'd made to reposition himself with Kyle inside the office; that bold move had almost gotten him caught. Once he was certain that Kyle was gone, he quietly stepped from behind the human size plant that set off in the corner of the room. He breathed a sigh of relief before taking a second to recheck the contents of his napsack ensuring the documents were within. Satisfied, he made his way towards the door and out of the office; deciding to leave the door unlocked again in order to toy with Kyle's mind again the following day.

Chapter Twelve

Kyle & Zoe

Zoe sat comfortably on the leather cushion couch inside the living room that she shared with Kyle. She was still in shock as she thought about Kyle's proposal and the fact that she was an engaged woman. Her heart was overwhelmed with happiness and she was filled with glee. She quickly began examining the engagement ring that was on her finger. She moved her hand from side to side, allowing the faucets to dance before her eyes. She had been waiting for this moment for years and she knew she deserved it. She really loved Kyle and wanted to build a family with him. She began to think about one day having children with him. How many would she give him? What would their names be? She personally wanted a boy and a girl but what would he want? Suddenly she began to feel an overwhelming sense of sadness overcome her. She couldn't understand where the sudden change of energy came from, but decided to focus her attention back on her future. If she had a son, she wanted him to be named after his father and she was sure that Kyle would want the same thing. If she had a daughter, she wasn't so sure what she would name her. Maybe she would let Kyle decide. Just then, the overwhelming sense of sadness overcame her once again but this time she realized why: Sasha.

The thought of having children again made her think of her deceased child. It had been ten years since the tragic car accident that claimed the lives of Sasha and Zoe's ex-husband, Steve. Zoe was finally coming to terms with it and was almost to the point that she no longer blamed herself for their departure. For years, it had haunted her because they were out driving in the middle of a snowstorm because they were looking for her. She had deserted them because of her infidelity and cowardice. Her leaving caused Steve to take to drinking heavily. He was three times past the legal limit the night of the accident and neither him nor Sasha had a chance at survival.

Zoe's thoughts were instantly interrupted as she heard her phone began to chime. She picked it up from the coffee table and answered it once she realized it was Kyle.

"Hey, babe" she answered with more sadness in her voice than she realized.

"Hey baby, what's wrong?" asked Kyle from the sound of Zoe's voice.

"Nothing" she replied.

"I can hear it, it's something. Do you want to talk about it?"

Zoe paused briefly while contemplating it. She really didn't want to put a damper into their conversation and ruin the high that they were both riding due to their engagement but then again, she knew that Kyle would want to know and that he would understand.

"I was just sitting here daydreaming of our future and I began to think about us and us raising a family and in the midst of my thoughts, I began to feel sadness for some reason, and I realized that reason was because thinking of having children made me think of Sasha and Wayne! I still can't believe that it's been ten years and sometimes I feel guilty that I'm moving on and that I no longer think about them as much as I used to. For some reason, I feel wrong" confided Zoe.

"There's nothing to feel wrong about, baby. Both Sasha and Steve understand that you love them, and they know that, for your sanity, that you have to continue to live your life. They both would want you happy, Zoe."

"I know but, I just don't know…" replied Zoe confused.

"Trust me when I say that neither Sasha nor Steve hold you responsible for what happened to them, and even if they did, they would tell you that they forgive you and have forgiven you a very long time ago. You have nothing to feel guilty about. You have to continue to live your best life and accept the faith that God has chosen for you and that would make Sasha and Steve happy" counselled Kyle sincerely.

"You're right" replied Zoe.

"Pick your head up, baby" encouraged Kyle.

"It's up" replied Zoe as a smile crept upon her face.

Kyle always had a way of making her feel better when she was down. He was genuine with his advice and she knew that he truly cared no matter what her problem was.

"Well, the reason why I'm calling is because I wanted to let you know that I have a surprise for you" informed Kyle.

"A surprise? What is it? Tell me" demanded Zoe impatiently.

"Slow down a little, Mrs. Impatient," replied Kyle with a laugh. "First, you got to tell me why you love me" demanded Kyle.

"Because you listen to me, you believe in me, you make me feel desired and needed. Because you make love to me so good, you are extremely handsome, you deal with my mood changes, you rub my feet and give me some of the best massages, because you help me out around the house, you cook for me, you watch corny movies with me…"

"Dang, stop jocking me" joked Kyle as they both broke out into laughter.

"What's the surprise?" asked Zoe anxiously after the laughter subsided.

"Get up and go to the hallway closet and look on the shelf."

Zoe quickly got up and ran down the hallway towards the closet with her phone in hand. Once there, she snatched open the door and got on her tippy toes to look on the shelf. She began throwing items off the shelf in search of a gift. "Where is it, I don't see anything" whined Zoe after finding nothing.

"Where are you?" asked Kyle.

"I'm in the hallway closet like you directed me."

"OH, did I say hallway closet? I meant to say look out the living room window."

"KYLE! Why do you play so much?" asked Zoe feigning annoyance as she quickly made her way back down the hallway and into the living room. She ran over to the window and snatched the curtain away and looked out into the driveway. What she saw next caused her to scream in joy. She quickly went to the door and into the driveway. Sitting before her was a black and white Rolls Royce wrapped in a large red ribbon. She quickly opened the door and jumped inside the driver's seat. The feel of the peanut butter brown leather that the seats were made of was against her skin. She began punching buttons after button as the vehicle lit up on the inside.

"Thank you, thank you so much, baby. I love you so much" screamed Zoe into the phone with so much excitement about having her dream car.

Before she knew it, tears began to fall from her eyes. She was overwhelmed with emotion from her happiness with Kyle and sadness from Sasha and Steve. "It's just an early wedding present for my queen. Zoe don't tell me that you're crying" replied Kyle with a bit of concern.

Zoe continued to let the tears pour as her emotions took hold. She couldn't believe how far along she came since Sasha in Steve's accident. She thought she would never get over the feeling of defeat she wanted to give up plenty of times and join them, but she kept her faith in the Lord and His plans and now she was in a complete state of bliss.

"Yes, I am" replied Zoe as she gained her composure. "But thanks to you these are tears of joy. I love you so much, Mr. Malone."

"I love you even more, my future Mrs. Malone." replied Kyle.

Chapter Thirteen

Arnold

The light steam seeping from the sewer in the dark alleyway did wonders to help conceal the identity of whoever decided to lurk there. The man standing in the shadows had his trench coat pulled tightly closed and the brim to his expensive leather hat pulled down over his eyes concealing him. He took a puff from his cigarette and exhaled adding to the smoke that already lingered. He hoped that the cigarette would help him forget what he was there to do. He shook his head in disgust at himself, but quickly dismissed it when he thought about what he was set to profit from his sin of betrayal. To some, the love of money was the root of all evil, but to him it was the root of all good things. He brought the cigarettes to his lips again, pursuing them tightly to hold it there before rubbing his hands together to draw heat.

With no luck, he quietly cursed his co-conspirator for being late. He figured the man did this to keep him at limbo and to keep control of this shady business they'd embarked upon together. Just then, an extra pair of bright headlights approached, revealing him before the driver killed the ignition giving the place back its inconspicuous touch and the man back his clear vision. The man took the time to brush the flame from the building, extinguishing it before licking out the truck again and watching his acquaintance slowly descend.

"How do you do, Mr. Simmons?" asked the man with his hand extended out to Arnold for a handshake.

"No names, remember?" Arnold took the time to remind the man before dismissing his hands without shaking it. Arnold understood that this was strictly business and knew that he was slithering in grass with a snake.

The man overlooked the apparent disrespect and again reminded himself of his purpose. "Yeah, righ…." began the man before Arnold rudely interrupted him. "Do you have the papers?" The man looked out at Arnold in contempt before hesitantly bending down in unlatching the bolts to his briefcase. He leafed through several important pieces before coming up on the papers that Arnold was inquiring about. "Here they--"

"Shut up", stated Arnold before snatching the papers away from the man before flipping through them.

The man stood and began to watch Arnold survey the material. After several minutes, Arnold finally looked away from the papers and into the man's eyes.

"Business politics is truly an inherently vicious world to be involved in" stated Arnold as he unconsciously repeated his father's words. He knew that when it came to business, the only thing that mattered at the end of the day was the bottom line and that was the very thing every businessman did everything in his power to protect. He looked at the man and seen greed seeping from his eyes in the way the stem was from the sewers. "You worthless gutter rat." Arnold whispered to himself.

"Excuse me?" the man asked.

"I said are you sure that this has all remained confidential, because I have no room for mishap. I'm sure you understand the consequences we--"

Now it was the man's turn to interrupt Arnold. "Everything is secure. Trust that I cross every T and dotted every I . I'm very good at what I do Mr. Si...." The man ended as he restrained himself from saying Arnold's name again. Arnold looked at him and couldn't understand how someone with an Ivy League education, a prominent position in finance, and so much promise for success could be so conniving and cutthroat; but then again, he really didn't care one way or another. All he wanted was to destroy a man that had once tried to destroy him. He thought about all the damaging information that the records showed. Even though the information was falsely recorded, he figured that it wouldn't be found out and it would achieve its goal.

"Okay, and are we still in agreement that the leak will happen in two months from the date?" asked Arnold of the man.

The man shook his head in agreement before bending down and relatching his briefcase. He grabbed a hold of it and looked around suspiciously one more time.

"Don't try to cross me, I'm sure I don't have to warn you of the consequences if you do, do I?"

Just as the man finished his statement, he felt Arnold's strong hands grip him around his windpipe lifting him off his feet and into the air, causing him to gasp for air. "Don't ever threaten me, do you understand?" After a while, Arnold reluctantly released his grip of the man's neck, causing the man to bend over while continuously gasping for air. Arnold took the documents into his briefcase and turned to get back inside his truck. He jumped inside before screeching off, leaving the man to wonder with whom he was getting himself involved.

Chapter Fourteen

Arnold & Erica

Erica rocked her hips from side to side as she danced around the house to Destiny's Child song "Cater to You." She had the house smelling good from the five-course meal that she cooked just for Arnold. She was lighting the candles that she had placed all around the house one by one to give the house a unique hue. She was in a good mood because he was set to be home soon. She really missed him and longed for his touch. She needed to be held and made love to seeing that it was such a long time since Arnold was able to fulfill her needs. She needed him and refused to allow him to neglect her on his trip home. She knew that she looked sensational in her white Victoria's Secret lingerie set with matching white Jimmy Choo heels. She felt it would make it impossible for him to resist her. She spent hours doing her makeup, spreading rose petals out and prepairing his meal in order to set a romantic mood. She dropped Arnold Jr. off at her parents' house so that she could spend the evening alone with her husband. She knew they needed the time to focus on nothing but themselves.

Ever since Arnold had become focused on the elevation of his newly acquired corporations, he barely had time to make it home. Erica knew how badly Arnold wanted these corporations to succeed, especially since he decided to give them his father's last name. This, she knew, is what fueled him; making his father's dreams come true. She knew that he was trying to channel all of his pain and energy into these businesses in order to help him cope with this father not being there. She told herself she must strive to be an understanding wife and to be considerate of the stress Arnold was enduring. The loss of his father would always be hard for him to fully accept. She hated that they had to accept the reality because she couldn't deny that she wanted him home more. She told herself to remain supportive, but part of her wondered how much longer she would be able to accept the loneliness before it became a serious problem.

She quietly hoped that he'd make the proper changes so that she wouldn't have to complain and appear inconsiderate. Her feeling neglected wasn't the only thing fueling her desire for him to be home more; it was also Arnold Jr.'s consistent crying for his father. There was only so much that she could do as a woman raising a growing son. She knew he needed his father in ways that she couldn't fulfill. She told herself that today she would get things to change a little. She would feed him well, massage him good and make love to him like never before and then afterwards she would carefully voice her concerns to him about his household feeling neglected.

After lighting the candles, she made her way over to the wine cellar and pulled out a bottle of their finest. She poured herself a flute before sitting down at the table and admiring the layout of the meal she'd prepared. She couldn't wait for Arnold to see all of her hard work, he was due home in a matter of minutes and just the thought of it made her moist between her legs. She needed his touch and attention more than ever. She slowly began to sip her wine while reflecting on their relationship. Overall, she was happy, and Arnold really turned out to be the husband that she thought he would be. He was protective of them and provided for them. Ever since they got married, Arnold spared no expense on their lifestyle. She looked around at the newly designed mansion that she'd convinced him to purchase and smiled to herself. This was her dream house and Arnold allowed it to be her own little project. She decorated it exactly how she wanted to, with an unlimited budget. She appreciated his generosity when it came to her and was thankful for it. She polished off her first glass of wine and poured herself another.

As she began to sip, she found herself unconsciously rubbing herself between the legs. The thought of her husband began to turn her on even more. She was extremely hot and moist. She couldn't wait for Arnold to walk through the door. As her thoughts began to consume her, her phone began to rain interrupting them, she answered once she realized it was Arnold.

"Hey, honey" she greeted excitedly.

"Hey baby, how are you and Jr. doing?" asked Arnold.

"Okay. Your son is with my parents and I'm home patiently awaiting your arrival."

"Oh…. well, see that's the reason why I'm calling. I won't be able to make it home for another couple of days. I was just introduced to a possible new client that has requested an immediate meeting" informed Arnold.

"So, you won't be home today?" asked Erica in disappointment.

"I'm so sorry, baby, this was all unexpected."

"Goddamnit, Arnold!" cursed Erica.

"Erica! Watch your language" reprimanded Arnold.

Erica stood up and began to pace. She really wanted to give Arnold a piece of her mind but thought better of it. She began taking several deep breaths, regaining her composure before speaking. "I apologize for my reaction, honey. Do what you need to do and call me when you can."

"Okay baby, thanks for being understanding. I love you" finished Arnold. "I love you, too" finished Erica before hanging up. She stopped pacing in the middle of the dining room, before she realized what she was doing she forcefully threw her wine glass against the wall, shattering it instantly. Her tears began falling immediately, leaving her feeling sexually frustrated and emotionally defeated.

Chapter Fifteen

Kyle & Zoe

Kyle and Zoe pulled up to the handsomely designed mini mansion owned by Zoe's parents on the outskirts of Selma, Alabama. They made their way out to the hot and humid city so that Kyle could finally meet Mr. and Mrs. Fields. He was eager for the visit because he wanted to have a conversation with Mr. Fields about marrying his daughter.

They walked up to the massive cherry wooden door and knocked before Kyle quickly straightened his attire making sure that he was presentable. The door flung open and before them stood a small, fragile older woman of about seventy. She was slightly tanned with grey-blonde hair falling loosely over her shoulders and emerald-green eyes that seemed to pierce right through them.

"Mom!" exclaimed Zoe as she reached and wrapped the fragile older woman into her embrace. Kyle could easily see the resemblance and could instantly recognize where Zoe had gotten her beauty from.

Zoe released her mother and began to introduce her to Kyle. "Mom, this is my fiancé, Kyle Malone. Kyle, this is my mom, Betty Fields."

"Nice to meet you, Mrs. Fields" Kyle reached his hand out to shake the older woman's hand. He noticed her hesitation and, if he wasn't mistaken, he thought he recognized a sense of distaste in her eyes. She reached her hand out and accepted the handshake. She quickly released his hand and gave Zoe a disapproving look. Kyle looked over at Zoe in hopes of a form of clarification, but it seemed she missed the moment.

"Where's Poppa?" asked Zoe about her father.

"He's off in the dining area, let's go greet him, shall we?" finished Mrs. Fields as she led the way.

"Poppa!" screamed Zoe excitedly as she ran to her father and hugged him tightly. Kyle stood off to the side and watched their interaction. Mrs. Fields stood slightly away from them glaring at him in a disapproving manner. Kyle glanced back at Mr. Fields who was an older man of about seventy-five that looked pretty fit for his age. He was tall with the broad shoulders of a military man. His hair had mostly thinned from time, leaving light grey stubble on top.

"Poppa" began Zoe. "I would like for you to meet my fiancé, Kyle Malone. Kyle, this is my father, Robert Fields."

"Nice to finally meet you, Mr. Fields" greeted Kyle as he reached his hand out for a handshake. Mr. Fields looked down at his hand without accepting it. He turned and addressed Zoe. "Fiancé?" Darling, he's a nigger."

"Excuse me?" said Kyle appallingly.

"Poppa! How rude of you!" reprimanded Zoe.

"Well excuse me dear, but I wasn't forewarned of this. I thought you had the right mind to date someone of your caliber."

"I do, that is exactly why I'm engaged to Kyle. Poppa, you're being extremely rude" finished Zoe.

"Am I not welcomed?" asked Kyle.

"No, son. I beg your pardon, I've just been caught off-guard, but since you're here with my daughter, of course you're welcomed" replied Mr. Fields unconvincingly.

The awkwardness lingered briefly before Mrs. Fields took the floor. "Well, since you're here, let you two make yourselves comfortable while I finish preparing the table."

Kyle tried to disregard the previous interaction as he prepared himself along with Zoe for supper. He hoped that the rest of the evening wouldn't have the same awkward result. He really wanted them to accept him and planned on talking with Mr. Fields about getting his blessings to marry Zoe. Once the meal was ready, they sat at the table and prepared to eat. Mrs. Fields went with a healthy platter of meatless lasagna, a Caesar salad and soft buttery garlic bread sticks. Kyle had to admit that the meal was delicious and the wine that accompanied it was of rare quality.

During dinner, Mr. Fields took the opportunity to talk as much as possible. He felt the need to tell Kyle about his experiences during his almost forty years with the Selma Police Department. He talked about when he'd first begun coming up in the ranks and the way he'd proven himself as a no-nonsense cop, especially toward the disruptive and disobedient Negroes. He discussed the beatings that he said he was forced to give so-called Negro revolutionist that were trying to corrupt their good country. He talked about as times changed how hard it was on the department having to integrate Negroes into their force. He accused the newly integrated Negroes of causing corruption within their department. He reminisced on what he referred to as the good ole times when the Negro knew their place and how society was so much better off that way. He talked and he talked until he was talking in circles. Finally, Zoe came to the rescue asking if they could all enjoy some dessert inside of the living room by the fireplace. By the time, Kyle's blood had begun to boil, and Zoe sensed his irritation.

Dessert was a peach cobbler that was light on sugar, but rather tasty. As they sat enjoying dessert, Kyle took small bites followed by huge gulps of his wine. He took notice to how Mr.

Fields was monitoring his consumption of the alcoholic beverage but paid it no mind, he figured the only way he'd get through this visit was if he was slightly intoxicated. After a while, Mr. Fields asked Zoe if he could please have a word with her in private. The moment Mr. Fields and Zoe were out of earshot, Mrs. Fields began her interrogation, "Kyle, is it?" asked Mrs. Fields.

"Yes, it's Kyle" replied Kyle nonchalantly. He felt slightly offended that he'd been in her home for several hours and she neglected to know his name.

"So where are you from, Kyle?" she asked.

"Chicago, Illinois."

"OH… Were you raised in one of those housing projects there?'

"No. My Big Momma and Poppa actually own our home. The house has been in our family for generations."

"So, are you one of the ones of your kind that was fortunate enough to finish high school?" Mrs. Fields continued.

"Yes, but I was more than fortunate enough to finish high school; I was first in my class at the University of Illinois. I've obtained my B.A. in business, majored in accounting and have minors in both economics and marketing" replied Kyle.

"Oh, so how'd you and our Zoe meet?" replied Mrs. Fields while trying to think up another angle.

"We met on business" he said.

"Were you working for her?"

"No, actually at the time, we both worked for the World National Bank. Myself as the lead accountant and Zoe as the marketing director" replied Kyle.

"So, do you still maintain employment there or have you become a statistic inside the staggering black unemployment rate?" she asked accusingly.

Kyle was taken aback by her line of questioning. He felt himself on the verge of losing his cool, but he somehow managed to maintain his composure. "No, I'm no longer employed through them" he replied.

"Uhm…" responded Mrs. Fields disapprovingly.

"But now I'm an equal partner and owner of Precise Accounts, which is the third largest accounting firm in Chicago. We manage accounts for major corporations such as Facebook, Amazon, Tyler Perry Studios, and Walmart, to name a few. We've had gross revenue upward of one hundred million dollars for three consecutive quarters and we're on the verge of becoming a household name" finished Kyle before standing to his feet. He asked Mrs. Fields in which direction was the restroom in, she pointed off in a direction without words as Kyle excused himself.

Kyle made his way down the long hall in search of the restroom. He was fuming and beyond pissed that Zoe had led him into this assault without warning. He continued to seek out the restroom, while doing so, he came across a bedroom that door was slightly ajar. Coming from within the inside of the room were hushed whispers of what appeared to be a heated argument. Kyle put his back to the wall just outside of the room and began to listen. "I thought you would approve of him, Poppa, he's a really good man and he treats me really well" he heard Zoe say.

"But he's a nigger, for crying out loud. I thought I raised you better than to succumb to the slums for a mate" he replied to her.

"You're talking like he's some sort of gutter rat. He's a brilliant, highly educated and respected man. Besides that, he takes really good care of me" she held on.

"I just don't understand why you didn't find someone more like Steve. He was a good man. He was well-educated in the history of the founders of this country and was proud of his race. I'm sure he's turned over in his grave witnessing your choice of a suitor."

"What—" responded Zoe in shock. "How dare you mention him in the context of this conversation? Have you no boundaries when it comes to your limited and simple conservative views?"

"Have you no boundaries in your choice of men? A negro for heaven's sake!" replied Mr. Fields in disgust.

Kyle decided that he heard enough as he finally made his way to the restroom. A part of him felt like he was going to regurgitate from the entire experience, but he refused to allow them to make him feel defeated. After pretending to use the restroom he made his way back toward the living room to join Mrs. Fields. Once there, he realized that Mr. Fields and Zoe had rejoined her.

"Get your things Zoe, it's time for us to leave" announced Kyle while standing tall. Zoe looked confused and Mrs. Fields appeared disappointed.

"Why so soon?" she asked, more to Zoe than to Kyle.

"It isn't soon enough…" replied Kyle before leading the way out.

Once they made it outside, Kyle took the time to properly address Zoe. "What the fuck was that all about?"

"What was what about?" Zoe asked, confused.

"You could've warned me that I was walking into an ambush."

"That was hardly an ambush" she responded.

"What exactly was it then? You could've forewarned me that your parents were living in the Jim Crow era" he replied, almost seething.

"My parents may be stubborn and may hold conservative views, but they didn't mean anything by it."

"The hell they didn't. Your mother looked at me as if I was there to rob their home. Your father refused to shake my hand and talked for hours about being a slave catcher. I felt like I was having dinner with Willie Lynch. I didn't know when I'd be led out back to be hung from a tree by your bigoted, disrespectful, simple-minded ass parents" he shot at her.

"Kyle, I would not stand here and allow you to refer to my parents in such a degrading way. You need to take that back or…" she replied, hurt.

"Kyle instantly interrupted Zoe, "or what?" he challenged her.

"Or I will not be heading back to Chicago with you if you cannot respect and accept my parents" threatened Zoe.

Kyle took a moment before replying. He looked deep into her eyes. He didn't recognize her and felt as if he was staring into the eyes of a complete stranger. Had she not heard the same things he'd heard? Was she that accustomed to that sort of rhetoric coming from her parents that she no longer considered it wrong? Was she really that oblivious to their disrespect and that insensitive to his feelings that she would side with her parents when clearly they were the ones in the wrong? Kyle looked deeper into her eyes and after realizing that they hadn't softened and still held the same defiance, he knew that it was time for him to leave.

"No" he stated before taking a couple of steps back from her. "Your parents are the ones who couldn't accept or respect me."

With that said he quickly turned and got inside of his car. He put the car into gear before speeding off without looking back without seeing the tears that were slowly trickling down Zoe's face.

Chapter Sixteen

Arnold & Erica

A rnold and Erica stood in the midst of the woodchucks that surrounded the swing set at the park that they were visiting with their son Arnold Jr. Arnold stood behind his son, who was seated comfortably in the swing slowly pushing him to his child like satisfaction.

"So, what you're saying is that you're going to fly to California again for almost a month?" ask Erica with extreme irritation.

"Listen, Erica, if I had a choice in the matter, I wouldn't be doing it."

"I'm not trying to nag you, Arnold, but you've only been home for three days. Most of that time has been spent inside of your office, now you're standing here telling me that you're going out of town again. Can't you assign the responsibilities to someone else?"

"The last time that I tried that, we got out-negotiated for a multimillion-dollar contract. I have yet to find someone with the ferocity to go into these meetings and win these crucial negotiations, and until I do, I'm forced to handle these things on my own" Arnold paused briefly while looking over Erica. He could sense the frustration coming from the look on her face.

"Erica, you knew that I was going to be overwhelmed with responsibilities once I took control of the companies. You said that you understood and that you support me, what has changed?"

"Nothing has changed. I just didn't know that it would come with the complete neglect of your family" stated Erica.

"Neglect, Erica? Really? You know that that isn't a fair evaluation" he replied.

"No, what isn't fair is me having to explain to our son why his father is never home to tuck him in at night and read a bedtime story. What isn't fair is me having to hear him say he doesn't want to eat his cereal in the morning unless you're the one pouring the milk. What isn't fair is…"

"Okay, okay—" interrupted Arnold. "I get your point, but I need you to understand mine. I'm swamped with all types of new responsibilities that I'm trying my hardest to succeed in. Do you really believe I don't want to be home more with you two? I'm stressed beyond belief not being able to make it home most nights."

"Your actions don't show that you want to be home with us" Erica said stubbornly.

"God damn it, Erica!" cursed Arnold in frustration.

"Owwww" Arnold Jr. interrupted. "Daddy just used a bad word" he said with a smile on his face.

"Watch your language around my child" stated Erica in a chastising manner.

"He's my child, too."

Arnold felt his temperature rising from Erica's lack of consideration. He was working hard, breaking his neck to maintain their lifestyle and to keep a luxurious roof over their heads. He was making sure that their son was able to attend one of the best private schools in the nation and finally he was keeping her credit card without a limit so that she could shop and indulge herself in shopping sprees. He was doing everything and yet she was still complaining.

"Erica, I need you to remember that all of our mortgage payments are expensive, the cost of private school goes up yearly and your designer garbs along with your taste for high-quality diamonds cost money; money that isn't made if I'm not working."

"Are you really using bills and my lifestyle as an excuse? You and I both know that the revenue brought in from Forever United in Forever Together was significant enough to pay all the bills. We never needed for you to take over these companies so that we could sustain our lifestyles and know that" stated Erica angrily.

"No, we didn't until you wanted a bigger house while we were still paying the mortgage on our other home here, our home in Chicago and our vacation home in Florida and let me not mention your impulsive shopping has increased tenfold."

"Huh. Are you really being serious right now? I'm standing here telling you that your son and I want you home more and you're trying to use bills as an excuse for your absence. You need to know that in order for our relationship to last and for our family to last you must make more time for us" she concluded.

"Did you just threaten me?"

"No! Could you please unplug your big ears for one second and hear what I'm asking from you?" stated Erica in frustration.

Arnold Jr. took the time to giggle. "Big ears…" Their son's amusement did little to ease the tension between them. Arnold felt like Erica was being inconsiderate of the circumstances. He felt that she forgot that she initially encouraged him to engage himself into the responsibility when he first won the verdict.

"Listen, Arnold, I know that initially I said I would be fine with you doing what you had to do, and I meant that to some degree. I honestly believed that you'd be able to find a balance. That's all I'm saying… is that I need you to find a balance between work and home."

"Don't you believe that I'm trying? I'm here as much as my schedule will allow." relayed Arnold in irritation.

"Then maybe you need to rearrange your schedule because we need you home more than two times a month. We can't keep living like this, Arnold. I'm getting sick and tired of your half of our bed being cold at night. It's getting lonely, Arnold. I'm your wife and I need you home to hold me at night."

"All I can tell you is that I'll try. I won't make any promises because I can't afford to neglect my work" he told her.

"You can afford to neglect your family, though, how ironic…" finished Erica while shaking her head. "Arnold, I know you may fear the risk of losing out on contracts if you're not hands-on, but I must inform you that you might risk losing your family if you don't become more hands-on at home."

"Erica, I will not tolerate you threatening me again" warned Arnold.

"That wasn't a threat, it was a promise" finished Erica, defiantly.

She stepped in front of the swing and stopped it. She picked their son up from the seat of the swing and put him in her arms. She stood in front of Arnold while glaring into his eyes. He returned her stare while trying to keep his composure. She felt that they were now at a crossroads. She loved him and valued him as a husband. She didn't want to seem unsupportive, she just wanted to feel loved and considered. It was hard being home basically raising their son alone and it was taking a toll on her. She felt like she deserved to be catered to at the end of the night after catering to their son throughout the day. The fact that she had to hold her pillow at night was unbearable. If Arnold couldn't understand where she was coming from then she would make good on her promise.

"A promise, huh?" asked Arnold.

Erica didn't reply as she turned on her heels with their son in tow. She headed back to the car leaving Arnold standing alone the way she promised he would be if he didn't find a balance between his work and his family.

Chapter Seventeen

Cante & Louis

"Hey, girl!" said Cante once Erica answered the phone.

"Hey!" responded Erica, matching her excitement.

"What are you doing?" asked Erica.

"Looking over some potential wedding gowns and bridesmaids dress, I never knew the process was so daunting" replied Cante.

"No girl, you're just picky" replied Erica.

"I mean, we only get one wedding, right? So, I might as well make it one to remember. Louis is leaving me in full control and said that the budget is unlimited!" Cante bragged.

"Must be nice. I still can't believe how far the two of you have come. I would have never imagined that you two would have been engaged" relayed Erica astounded.

"I guess we can't control destiny. Honestly, I never imagined myself committing to one man. Just the thought of it used to bore me half to death, but with Louis, it's always new and exciting. He's so thoughtful and he understands me. He knows that I have a short attention span so he's always finding new and creative ways to keep my attention and interest."

"Wow, are you talking about the same Louis that I know? If so, Cante you really have changed that man into something totally different" replied Erica.

"No, I just believe that it took for him to meet someone who could be compatible with him for him to slow down and show that part of him. It's always been in him because he does all of these things without me telling him to. He knows when I want to be left alone and he also knows when I don't want to be alone. He listens to the things that I don't say. This is the very first time I had a man who understands that he has two ears and one mouth for a reason. Girl, it feels so good to be considered and understood." finished Cante happily.

"Must be nice" replied Erica, a bit more sadly than she intended. She didn't want to rain on Cante's parade. She remembered the times that Arnold was the exact same way. Not only did it seem like they weren't only not on the same page, but they weren't even in the same book.

"Girl, you know how nice it is. Arnold's been this man to you for years."

"He was that kind of man to me for years. Now, it's like I don't know."

"OMG… Erica, what's been going on?" asked Cante.

"Don't allow me to spoil the mood" she responded.

"Girl, stop it. Your problems are mine. You can never spoil my mood, now tell me what's been going on" announced Cante concerned.

"Huh, girl. So, you know that Arnold won the civil suit granting him ownership of several companies. Well, he's taking on the responsibility wholeheartedly. Now, I've always supported Arnold and his ambition, and this time is no different. I will still support him, I just assumed that I wouldn't be the only one being considerate in this situation. I believe that he would be able to find a balance between home and work. A balance that would allow him to continue to excel in his ventures, but also be able to give myself and Arnold Jr our time. But I was wrong about that because he's rarely home and when he is, he's cooped up in that damn office of his" vented Erica.

"When you addressed him concerning this, what did he say?"

"He missed my point entirely. It was like I was speaking a foreign language to him. He said I was being inconsiderate and that I knew of the responsibility he was taking on beforehand. Then he started saying that because I wanted a new home and we still wasn't finished paying off our other homes and because my shopping sprees increased tenfold that he has to work so much to fund these expenses…" Erica continued.

"No, he didn't!" responded Cante disbelievingly.

"The audacity of the man! All I wanted was for him to understand that his son wants him home more, and so do I. Arnold Jr admires that man and acts as if I'm not good enough sometimes and that his father is the only thing that he needs. Not to mention how long I've been left to feel like I'm raising a child during the day and dating myself during the night. I don't like this feeling, Cante" stated Erica.

"Yeah, girl… he needs to get it together. He needs to understand that he's not married to his job, he's married to you and you as a woman needs tender loving care."

"Exactly," Erica agreed. "I've almost forgotten what his touch feels like."

"So, when he's home, he's not making love to you?" asked Cante.

"The only loving I've been getting is from B.O.B." Erica replied.

"Don't tell me that you've been cheating…" gasped Cante.

"No! Cante, BOB is my battery-operated boyfriend" she replied.

Cante laughed at this revelation. "Oh, girl I was about to give you the third degree. So, do you think he's…" Cante's paused not wanting to ask the question.

"Do I think that he's what?" "Cheating?"

"No! Of course, not Cante. Arnold could get lost in work, but not that lost. I don't believe that Arnold has a deceptive bone in his body. Besides, that man knows he'll be my first 187 if he did something of the sort" said Erica.

"My bad girl, no need in getting all Snoop Dogg on me." They both laughed at this.

"So, what are you going to do to get things back on solid ground with him?" asked Cante.

"It's not up to me to fix things. He's the one with the issues, I did warn him that if he didn't start making myself and his son a priority that he'd find himself alone." relayed Erica.

"Which you should've."

"Yeah, but girl, I can't wait till your wedding," said Erica, wanting to change the subject. "I know that you're going to be the most beautiful bride ever and Louis will make a handsome groom. Not to mention I'll be the most beautiful bridesmaid ever."

"Yeah, and Kyle will be a handsome best man."

Erica became quiet after Cante's last statement. "I'm sorry, Erica, that kind of slipped out," she apologized.

"It's okay" Erica said before pausing briefly,

"So, he's going to be there?" Erica asked after a while.

"How does that make you feel?" asked Cante as an answer.

Erica couldn't reply right away as she thought about it. She wasn't sure exactly how seeing Kyle again would make her feel. Even though she was married now, she couldn't deny the fact that he still crossed her mind on occasion. Seeing how things had turned out the last time they had seen one another she couldn't help but to wonder how he would respond to seeing her. She often wondered where life had taken him since then in the fact that he shied away from social media, he left her with no way to find out unless she asked Cante, which she refused to do. She felt that she was best keeping and thinking these things to herself. "Who cares?"

"Honestly, I don't feel one way or another" lied Erica. Cante could sense that Erica wasn't telling the truth, but thought it was wise to change the subject.

"Girl, we are going to have a ball!" she announced excitedly.

"I can't wait" said Erica. "So, what else have you been up to, girl?" she asked.

"Modeling and allowing Louis to fuck my brains out" she replied.

"TMI, girl, I don't want to hear about your sexcapades with Louis nasty self."

"Just an FYI, it's good!"

"Girl, tell me about the modeling," said Erica as they both broke into laughter.

After Cante composed herself, she began telling Erica about her up-and-coming runway appearances. She was to have three trips down the runway as the feature model: modeling some of the highest fashion. After she was done, Erica said "I wish I could be there, girl."

"It's okay, I'll tell you all about it. You just focus on getting through to Arnold's thick head" replied Cante.

"Yeah, I know? I love the man to death, but I refuse to allow myself to be mistreated and neglected" said Erica.

"Which you should never" Cante agreed.

"Well girl, Imma let you go. I can hear Arnold Jr. running all through my house. He's probably hanging from the ceiling fan as we speak" joked Erica.

"Okay girl, kiss my handsome nephew for me, will you?" said Cante.

"Of course, and congrats again on everything. Louis is a very lucky man" said Erica.

"I know, I tell him that all the time" said Cante seriously.

"Bye, girl" said Erica as she laughed. "Love you."

"Love you also" said Cante before ending the call.

Chapter Eighteen

Kyle and Louis

Kyle sat up on the bench after racking the weights back onto the bench press. He was sweating profusely, but seemed to still be filled with energy. Louis made his way to the bench aside Kyle and sat down. "Whatever those weights did to you I guarantee you they would never do it again" joked Louis.

Kyle didn't reply as he grabbed his towel and dabbed at his forehead with it. After slinging the towel over his shoulders, he seemed to go deep into thought, allowing his eyebrows to furrow. Louis watched his friend and could easily sense that something was racking his brain. He gave Kyle a minute with his thoughts before asking, "You wanna talk about it?"

Kyle looked up at Louis as if he'd just noticed that he was there for the first time. Before Louis knew what was happening Kyle began venting.

"The nerve of the woman to put me in that type of situation. I mean, she had to know what type of people her parents were and the type of reaction they would have towards me being in their home. On top of that, her mother talking to me and interrogating me like I'm sort of a second-class citizen, and then her father," Kyle paused briefly as if he was reliving the moment.

"I wish I could've taken him out back and put these hands to him. The racist, simple-minded, lack of a man. A nigger, could you believe he referred to me as that? I haven't been referred to as that in my face in years" vented Kyle.

"I didn't even know people still used the word" Louis said shocked.

"That's what I'm saying. For a second, I felt like I was thrown back sixty years in time. Then the man had the nerve to give me an entire history lesson on his involvement in everything short of lynches. I mean, he talked for hours like I wasn't part of the discussion. He acted as if somehow, I was out of place and needed to be reminded of my correct place. I've never been belittled that way."

"So, what did Zoe have to say about this?" asked Louis.

"She told me that she wouldn't allow me to speak of her parents in such a way." Kyle responded.

"She sided with them? Did she not hear the conversation that you're describing to me?" Louis continued.

"That's what I'm saying. How could she possibly side with them after everything that was said. I even kept my composure out of respect for her because I almost flipped out several times. I did this for her, and she couldn't even have my back after it was all said and done" voiced Kyle disgusted. "What hurts is I thought she cared enough about my feelings to at least show compassion. She acted as if the love for her parents was the only love that she had in her heart."

"Damn, bro. I would think Zoe would've corrected them at some point to let them know how much she cared for you," Louis said as he couldn't believe that Zoe hadn't stuck up for Kyle.

"Truthfully, bro, after her mom had interrogated me, I excused myself to the bathroom. On the way there, I overheard Zoe talking to her father and he was telling her how he thought she had more sense than to date someone like me and how her late husband is probably turning over in his grave from her choice of a suitor."

"So, what was her response?" Louis pressed on.

"Well, she told him that I'm a good man and that she thought he would like me. She told him that he was being extremely inappropriate for talking to me in that manner," Kyle finished.

"Hold on, so she did stick up for you?" asked Louis, a bit confused.

"Behind closed doors, she didn't even know that I heard them."

"Does that matter if she stuck up for you in the open or behind closed doors, Hell I'd much rather see how someone feels about me when they don't know I could hear them rather than when I'm present" Louis told Kyle.

"Yeah, but this was all before the fact. After I overheard them, I came out and told Zoe it was time to leave. Once we got outside, that's when she decided to stay there with them rather than to leave with me" Kyle replied.

"Maybe that was her first time going through something like that and she didn't know how to handle it properly. People make mistakes, bro" Louis advised.

"Right, and sometimes you have to make people learn from their mistakes and that's why I've refused to answer any of her texts or calls" Kyle responded.

"Do you think that's the best way to handle it?" asked Louis.

"It's the only way to handle it right now. If I just forgive her like it's nothing, then she'll continue to think it's nothing. I need her to see how it is to be with her parents without me since they're who she chose" stated Kyle stubbornly.

"I bet if you gave her a do-over right now this entire situation would have different results."

"There's no such thing as do-overs" Kyle snapped.

"So, you'd rather allow her to hurt and hurt yourself than to sit and talk this over with her?"

Kyle just shook his head in confirmation.

"That's being immature and stubborn, bro."

"She was both those things first," said Kyle.

"Two wrongs don't make…." Kyle interrupted Louis.

"I know, I know, but I'm willing to hurt myself for a period of time in order for her to learn life lessons."

Louis just shook his head disapprovingly. Together, they both just sat quietly while entertaining their own thoughts.

"So, how's things going with Cante?" Kyle asked.

"Great, she's super-excited planning the wedding, and honestly, I'm just as excited" relayed Louis gleefully.

"That's great" said Kyle more unenthusiastically than he'd intended.

"Sorry, bro, I know what you're going through, didn't mean to rub it in."

"Naw, you're good. I didn't mean to rain on your parade. I really want to hear more, bro" Kyle went on.

"Are you sure?" Louis asked.

"Of course, bro," said Kyle while giving a convincing smile.

"I mean, I've been doing everything in my power to make her happy and to keep her happy. I'm still learning as the days go about love and how I want to be. It's actually kind of fun experimenting and trying new things. I guess I have the basic sense of how it's supposed to go, so certain things I know better than to do but I try different things with surprising her and treating her to different things. I never knew anything could feel this good. Besides that, she treats me well and the sex is tremendous. I've never felt something so tight, wet and hot as her..." Kyle interrupted Louis, "Bro, bro, bro. Spare me the details, please I don't want these images in my head of Cante."

"Are you sure? Because...."

Again, Kyle interrupted. "I'm more than positive bro, but I'm happy for you. So when is the wedding?"

"I don't know the exact date at this minute but it's gonna be a destination wedding, so have your passport ready, my best man."

"You're giving me the honor of being your best man?" Kyle asked.

"Who else would I choose, fool? Hell, Cante chose Erica as her maid of honor.... Damn...my bad, bro" stated Louis forgetting how touchy of a subject Erica was to Kyle.

"It's cool bro. I'm over that. But she's gonna be there, huh?"

Louis just nodded his head "yes". Kyle grew quiet, thinking about how it will feel to run into Erica again. He wondered Would she have Arnold with her as well? Louis saw his friend overthinking, so he interrupted his thoughts.

"So, what's your next move with Zoe?" he asked.

"Just continuing to give her space until I'm ready to move past this and until I'm sure she's learned her lesson, but enough about that, it's your set, bro," finished Kyle as he got up and prepared to spot Louis.

Chapter Nineteen

Kyle

Kyle sat at the desk in his office with a confused and frustrated expression on his face. For some reason, their trial balance refused to balance. He began to go back over his steps to see if he missed anything. Realizing that he hadn't, he closed his books. He got up from his desk and began pacing the floor. Something wasn't right; something was terribly off. His office phone began to ring. He ignored it as he continued to pace the floor. He didn't want to be bothered with anything or anyone until he figured out the issue with their accounts. It wasn't a slide or transposition; it wasn't a transaction that was recorded in the wrong account; he couldn't figure it out as his phone began to ring again. He pulled out his cell phone and called Alu to try and get some clarity as to why their accounts refused to balance. Just then, Susan unexpectedly barged into his office with a concerned and urgent look on her face. The sight of her caused Kyle to tuck his cell phone back into his pocket.

"I apologize for barging in on you, Mr. Malone, but I've been calling you consistently in order to inform you that the representatives from the IRS and the SEC are requesting an immediate meeting and they're not taking no for an answer" ended Susan with panic and her voice.

"Okay" replied Kyle. "Send them in."

He was visibly confused as to why the IRS and the SEC would just show up at his office. They weren't due for a routine audit for at least six months. He gathered his composure before making his way back to his desk to take a seat. Only seconds later did the two representatives enter his office. After introductions were made, the two men took seats.

"So, what brings you gentlemen all this way on such short notice?" Kyle asked once everyone was situated.

"Well…" began the heavy-set representative who spoke with a lisp which did little to undermine his serious demeanor. "I would like to begin by apologizing for intrusion, but I'm sure you realize that this must be an urgent matter if we're here without warning" the representative paused briefly to allow his words to take effect. He hoped that his tone would highlight the seriousness of their visit and possibly frighten Kyle out of exposing the demon that he was convinced was hidden in his closet. "I'll get straight to the point, our department have been noticing some strange activity within several of your accounts lately" informed the representative blatantly.

"What exactly do you mean by strange?"

"Like fictitious accounts, fictitious transactions, no real receipts, no trace of any real corporations to have the need for these accounts; you know all the illegal mumbo jumbo that you guys like to engage in" finished the other representative after cutting in. His Southern drawl was thick, and Kyle instantly caught the accusation oozing from it.

"Do you have any records of these accounts that are in question?" asked Kyle while still maintaining his composure and professionalism.

The Southern representative took the time to dig through his briefcase for what seemed like an eternity before finally extracting the papers. He hesitated briefly while trying to think up something bravado to say, not being able to, he finally handed over the information.

Kyle began to look over the evidence, reading over every page carefully and thoroughly. He immediately began to recognize that some form of fraud was taking place. He also immediately began to realize who was responsible for it. He decided to appear naive to the fact but would try to get whatever information that he could from the investigators. "When did these transactions begin to appear?" he asked the representative rhetorically.

"I'm sure you can see from the headings of the financial statements that are in front of you" stated the heavyset representative slightly annoyed. "Listen, Mr. Malone, we can sit here and play mind games all day long and neither one of us would get anywhere or we could call a spade a spade and come to a conclusion" he finished.

Kyle looked over at the representative and gained a bit of respect for him and his intelligence in the moment. The main clearly knew his business and wasn't there to play games. He had a demeanor of an auditor who had nailed a scammer or two in his day. That auditor must have read his mind. "Now Mr. Malone, as you can see, I'm no rookie. With that being said, I want you to know that I can recognize a thief and scammer from a mile away and I don't recognize that in you. Now I can't say the same of your business acquaintances…." the representative paused briefly, allowing the hint to linger in the air.

"Mr. Malone, I understand where your loyalty lies, but I'm sad to inform you that it's misplaced. The accounts in that file are just the beginning of the fraud we've detected. We have information concerning the unexplained loss of gains from some of the accounts that you've had since your forming. Millions' worth of losses, Mr. Malone" the representative allowed his words to play on Kyle's mind.

Kyle began to kick himself from the revelations. He admitted to himself that he'd gotten caught slipping and, in the world of finance, one false move could cost you millions. In this case, it was also costing him a friend. Why would he be stealing and creating false accounts? Or better yet, he knew that he was supposed to have recognized this long ago. He had allowed what he'd been going through with Zoe to throw him off his square and the fact that he was trusting help to blind him as well. He made the mistake and neglected to assign separate people to handle cash and receipts, which are proper accounting practices. He thought Alu had their company's best interest at heart, but now he was able to see that he didn't.

None of the accounts that were being presented to him were in their original ledger, so there must've been a completely falsified ledger. He also knew that it would be hard to prove that he had no knowledge of the discrepancies. Instead of going back-and-forth, he decided to end his conversation with the investigators. He handed them his lawyer's contact information before showing them out of his office. After the investigators exited, he called his attorney and informed him about the auditors' possible visit to him. His mind was still in disbelief. He really couldn't believe the betrayal. He refused to allow it to cause them to crumble. He began to contemplate on how to make the best out of the situation. He needed to expose his business partner and he knew exactly how; it was his turn to create a false account, one that only he and Alu would know about.

Chapter Twenty

Cante & Louis

The lights shined brightly throughout the packed venue that held everyone from designers to investors, to celebrities and paparazzi. They were there to watch the highly anticipated fashion show that was being held in Chicago, Illinois for the very first time. Louis sat in the front row witnessing the consistent flicking and flashing that was coming from the cameras, giving the room a surreal look. He looked around and noticed several business tycoons, fashion moguls, and models that he knew personally. Everyone had come out to witness some of the most gorgeous models in the world fashioning some of the most high-priced garbs around. The lights in the venue went from brights to shade as model after model began to grace the runway.

Louis couldn't help but to acknowledge the beauty and grace of the woman and he was totally intrigued by a few, but he curtailed his thoughts and put them back onto his fiancée. He was here to support Cante on her first runway appearance. A smile crept up on his face from the thought of Cante. He knew that she was unmistakably the most beautiful model there and he was proud to say that she was his. He couldn't wait to watch her as she ripped the runway. She was set to take three trips down the runway in the first was only moments away. Louis uncrossed his legs briefly before crossing again in nervous anticipation.

"Ladies and gentlemen, let's welcome Cante in her first appearance of the night modeling a two piece Louis Vuitton swimsuit that is set to be available nationwide after tonight" announced the host of the event. Louis stood up once he noticed Cante approaching the stage. He watched in awe as Cante strutted confidently down the runway. The attendees begin to clap as soft chatter began about how sexy Cante made the two-piece look. Once Cante made it to the end of the runway, she posed seductively to give everyone the perfect view of the swimsuit as well as her well-sculpted body. She turned and strutted back up the runway as the flash from the cameras shined throughout. After Cante departed from the stage, Louis sat back down. He began to scan through the photos that he took on his phone of Cante. Suddenly, a business email from Kyle popped up on his screen and it read:

"Just got a visit from a representative from both the IRS and the SEC. They both notified me that several accounts didn't balance, false transactions recorded, money missing and understated. They have also been false accounts created. It seems that Alu isn't as loyal as we initially believed. Call ASAP so that we can discuss what's next."

Louis closed out the message and sat stunned in disbelief. His mind began to run rampart from the revelations and implications. Was Alu seriously committing fraud against the very company that he help form? Was he really embezzling money and falsifying documents? How could that be when together the three of them were making money hand over fist? Together they build their company up to become one of the top in the state, so that would possess Alu To act so irrational? He didn't want to believe the allegations but the fact that the IRS and SEC were seriously investigating them gave validations to the accusations. Even so, he couldn't understand the logic behind Alu's decision.

Louis heard Cante's name called again for her second trip down the runway, He tried to focus his attention on her. Cante's second trip was a bit of a blur to Louis as his mind couldn't get away from the news that he just heard. He began to think about the fact that Kyle had started to complain about a lot of things not adding up in their accounts. Initially, he'd just blamed it on the fact that Kyle was probably overwhelmed with all of the responsibility that was bestowed upon him, and to the fact that he knew Kyle's mind was distracted behind what he'd been going through with Zoe. He regretted not taking heed of Kyle's warnings, especially since he knew that Kyle was really good at his position.

"Fuck" whispered Louis to himself. "Why Alu?" he questioned. Again, he was broken from his thoughts as he heard Cante's name being announced for her walk down the runway which was also the finale. He focused on Cante and again found himself in a state of awe at Cante's ability to rock the runway. She wore a see-through Victoria's Secret nightgown that left little to the imagination and made every woman in attendance envious of her flawless body and made every man quietly fantasize about having her body against his.

Cante strutted confidently down to the end of the runway and paused in a seductive pose to allow the cameramen to capture her beauty before turning to make her way back up the ramp. On her way back, she seemed to stagger slightly and unexpectedly before catching her balance. She regained her composure and tried to continue her walk, but she staggered again, but this time she wasn't able to catch her balance as she collapsed face-first onto the ramp.

"Cante!" screamed Louis. He made it from his seat and jumped onto the stage as he ran toward Cante. He made it over to her and knelt down to her before scooping her into his arms.

"Cante, Cante, baby wake up" he said to her in a voice filled with panic. Cante's body lie motionless in his arms and she was unresponsive.

Chapter Twenty-One

Cante & Louis

"She's really sick" were the only words Louis spoke to Kyle once he walked up to him in the hospital. They stood right outside Cante's room staring at her through the glass window that was attached to the room. She looked weak and fragile while attached to all the machines and tubes. Kyle placed his hand on his friend's shoulder in a comforting way. Louis' head hung low as he fought to contain the tears that threatened to fall.

"What's the diagnosis?" asked Kyle concerned.

"They haven't informed me yet. They're still running tests to figure everything out. I don't understand, bro, she appeared to be healthy one minute and then the next she was unconscious" Louis stated sadly. He was on the verge of breaking down and was trying his hardest not to. His normally broad and erect posture was now sunken, leaving him with a defeated look. He just couldn't understand how and why this was all happening to Cante.

"Do you think that she could be dehydrated or overwhelmed?" asked Kyle.

"I asked that already, but the doctor is saying there's no way to be certain until all of the tests are complete. Honestly, I believe it is more drastic than that. The doctor says that he believes it's something internal because her basic vital signs are fine. That's the reason they have to run more extensive testing" said Louis.

"I'm sorry, bro" stated Kyle.

"Louis!" said a voice that came up from behind them. "Is she okay?"

Kyle and Louis turned toward the voice and, once they saw who it was, Kyle' heart instantly dropped. The woman instantly stopped in her tracks after noticing Kyle standing beside Louis.

"No, she is not doing well" informed Louis to Erica.

Erica wasn't sure she'd heard what he'd said because she was stuck in a trance while staring into Kyle's eyes. Kyle was also frozen in time as he stared back into the dark brown eyes that once held his heart. He tried to break eye contact, but he couldn't. It had been such a long time since they were in one another's presence and neither one knew exactly how to respond. Kyle finally broke their eye contact and looked at Erica. She was thicker than he'd last remembered, but it fit her well. Erica brought her eyes back over and up to the window of Cante's hospital room and looked in. She stared at her best friend briefly asking Louis for the diagnosis, never bothering to take her eyes away from her best friend.

"They haven't come with one yet, they're still running tests" he informed her.

Louis' mind was all over the place with worry for Cante. Erica held the same concern and hoped and prayed that her friend wasn't facing a terminal illness. She looked over at Kyle and couldn't help feeling nervous about being back in his presence. After a while, Louis excused himself so that he could go sit at Cante's bedside. Erica stood still while continuing to stare in onto her best friend that was in such a vulnerable state. Kyle stood beside Erica staring in on Cante. "I really hope that she's going to be okay" he stated sincerely. Erica didn't reply because she really didn't know how to.

Kyle continued, "It would really break Louis' heart if it is something serious" he finished.

"Mine, too" replied Erica.

They both became quite again as they looked in on Cante and Louis.

Eventually, Erica looked at Kyle, briefly examining him for any dramatic changes in his appearance. She noticed that he'd put on a few pounds, but they were mostly in his chest and arms. She just as quickly took her eyes away from him, feeling slightly guilty for checking him out.

"You know I never got the chance to apologize to…" Erica began, but was interrupted by

Kyle. "You don't have to apologize."

"Yes, I do Kyle, so can you please let me finish?" She looked over at Kyle who didn't protest. "I want to apologize for my role in how things went down the last time that we seen one another. I didn't mean for you to get hurt and I've felt guilty about that ever since" finished Erica.

"I understand, but I was equally at fault. I knew that I was playing with fire and understood that there was only one way a situation like that could've ended and that was badly. I hope you know that I never held a grudge against you for your part in things. We were both acting on confused emotions. It was just a lesson learned" finished Kyle as he looked at Erica.

Erica looked deeply into his eyes before breaking eye contact so that she could look back in on Cante.

"So, how have you been?" asked Erica sheepishly.

"All over the place" replied Kyle, more sadly than he'd wanted to let on.

"In what ways, if you don't mind me asking."

Kyle thought a second before replying. He didn't know whether he should be up front with her or not. He debated if he should keep it casual or should he let her in about everything he'd been going through with Zoe. He knew what he'd be risking by getting personal with her considering how things had turned out the last time they traveled down that road.

"Business has been treacherous. I guess the saying is true, more money, more problems" he finished intentionally omitting the more personal problems that he'd been dealing with.

Erica could sense that there was much more plaguing his mind. She knew that he could be extremely brief when he didn't want to discuss certain things.

"How about you?" asked Kyle.

"Life is a challenge. I finally understand what my father used to mean when he'd say don't be too quick to grow up because once you do, you'll wish you were a kid again" replied Erica.

"Isn't that the truth? The good ole' times before we knew what bills and love was" finished Kyle as he opened himself up to her.

"So, there is more to your all over the place' than just business?" asked Erica knowingly. She looked over at Kyle with anticipation etching her face, she knew that she was out of line for prying the way that she was, but since she felt it in his energy that something more was weighing him down, she couldn't help but ask.

Kyle placed his hands inside his pockets as he contemplated her line of questioning. He didn't understand why she was inquiring about personal matters. He knew that she understood the thin line that they would always be walking whenever they were in one another's company. He also knew how vulnerable he was at the moment and knew that it would be easy to find comfort in her words, but he also knew it would amount to no good. He felt that she had a lot weighing her down as well. He figured to himself that love must've been kicking her ass just as much as it was kicking his. Even though he wanted to, he knew that it wasn't for them to discuss their problems with one another. Besides that, his loyalty and love were still for Zoe, even though they were having problems. He knew that it would be deemed betrayal to discuss their problems with his ex-lover.

"I really hope that she gets better. It would hurt a lot of people if not" he said before pausing briefly to take a few steps back and away from the window. "It has been really nice seeing and talking to you, Erica. I hope you know that I still pray for you and for your happiness and I forever will" he finished before turning on his heels and heading out of the hospital leaving Erica alone as she continued staring in on Cante and Louis.

Chapter Twenty-Two

Kyle & Zoe

Zoe stood in front of her full-length mirror examining herself. She wore a full-length form-fitting Versace dress with black and gold Versace heels to match. She had her long blonde hair pulled into a tight ponytail just the way she knew Kyle loved. It had been weeks since she'd made the mistake of siding with her parents rather than with Kyle. She still couldn't believe that she'd made that mistake. She'd been beating herself up over that decision since it happened. She'd tried texting and calling Kyle in order to reconcile since it happened, but he refused to answer. She'd left messages at his office, through mail and on his voicemail, but still received the same results. She'd been sick with regret and her heart was hurting tremendously. She loved Kyle with all of her heart and didn't want to be without him. She had plans on going into his office to see him and to right her wrong. After she was satisfied that her appearance was perfect, she made her way out the house and into her car. Thirty minutes later, she was standing outside of Precise Accounts readying herself to enter. She couldn't believe that she had butterflies in her stomach as she stepped inside Precise Accounts and made it over to the elevator. She stepped in and before she knew it, she was on Kyle's floor. She stepped out and made her way to Susan. "Hello, Susan, how are you?"

"Hello, Ms. Fields, I'm doing fine and how about yourself?"

"I'm doing alright. Is Kyle in right now?" asked Zoe nervously.

"Yes, but he informed me that he didn't wish to have any visitors" relayed Susan hesitantly.

"Well, I'm sure he wasn't referring to me when he made that request. I'm actually hoping to surprise him so I would really appreciate it if you would give me a spare key."

"Ms. Fields, he actually said he didn't want any visitors and that included you."

"Are you sure he said me, specifically?" asked Zoe.

"Well, specifically he said no one and that included Mr. Johnson, Mr. Francis, and you. So, it wasn't just you, specifically" relayed Susan cautiously.

"Okay. So, can I ask you to phone him and let him know that I'm in the lobby and would love to have a quick word with him?"

"Yes, just give me a second" said Susan as she picked up her phone from the desk and dialed his extension. "Yes, Mr. Malone, I'm sorry to bother you, but Ms. Fields is here in the lobby and she's requesting a minute of your time, would you like for me to send her back? Oh, okay, can you hold on a second while I deliver your message? Okay, hold on. Ms. Fields, he wanted me to inform you that he didn't wish to see anyone at the moment."

Zoe looked over at Susan with a frustrated and hurt look on her face. She couldn't believe Kyle was still refusing to see or talk to her. Before she realized what she was doing she'd snatched the phone from Susan's hand, causing Susan to gasp out in shock.

"Kyle, this is Zoe, please don't hang up" she paused briefly to make sure that the line hadn't gone dead. Realizing it hadn't, she continued. "Kyle, I understand that I screwed up and I regret it. I don't know what had come over me or what even possessed me to leave you hanging the way that I did, but Kyle, I love you and really need to see you." She paused again to see if he would respond. Once he didn't and she realized that he hadn't hung up, she continued. "Kyle, what do I need to do? I'm hurting without you, I can't think, eat, or sleep. I don't have the energy to do anything but think about you and regret what I did. Kyle, I need you, can you please forgive me?" Tears began to well up in her eyes, she felt her heart beating rapidly and her legs feeling weak.

"Go home, Zoe."

"Huh? Kyle?" Zoe said again just as she heard the line go dead.

She looked across the desk at Susan just as her tears began to fall. Susan gave her the saddest look before reverting her eyes down at the countertop, feeling sad for Zoe. "Can you please phone him back?" Zoe asked Susan. Susan shook her head in the affirmative before picking up the phone and dialing again. She didn't get an answer and then tried three more times, achieving the same result. She looked up at Zoe with the saddest look before telling her that he wasn't answering. Before she could finish her sentence, Zoe had begun making her way towards Kyle's office.

"Wait a minute, you can't go back there!" Susan warned her as she followed Zoe. Zoe was almost there when Susan caught up to her and softly grabbed ahold of her arm. Zoe turned on her heels as Susan released her. She stared Susan in the eyes. "Listen, Susan, woman-to-woman, I really need you to go back to your desk. I really need to see this man and I'm not taking 'no' for an answer. So again, woman-to-woman, can you please go back to your desk?" Susan looked at Zoe as her tears caused her makeup to stain her face and thought about protesting before she turned on her heels and headed back to her desk.

* * * * *

Kyle walked over to his office window after hanging up on Zoe and began to peer out of it. He heard his office phone ring several more times, but refused to answer. He hated what was happening between him and Zoe and hearing the pain in her voice hurt him more than she would ever know. He'd been hurting every day since they separated. He didn't want to be without Zoe, she was the best thing that had happened to him since Erica. He had thought that he would never find another woman that would compare to Erica, but Zoe had proved him wrong. No, she wasn't perfect, she had her flaws just like anyone else, but he knew that she truly cared for and loved him. He wanted so badly to put his pride to the side and go after Zoe to let her know everything he'd been going through over her. He wanted to go tell her how hard it has been not answering her call, how hard it was to sleep at night without her next to him and how incomplete he felt without her touch. He wanted to tell her that he felt exactly the way that she did. She wasn't the only one going through it he wanted to tell—*Boom! Boom! Boom!*

Kyle's thoughts were immediately interrupted from the sound of someone pounding on his office door. He turned from his office window toward his door wondering what was going on.

"Kyle, open the door! Kyle!" Zoe screamed out frantically. She tried the doorknob again hoping that it was open this time. With no luck she knocked on the office door again. She couldn't believe what she was doing, but she could no longer control herself. Love had her acting irrationally and she didn't care. She needed to see her man more than anything.

"Kyle!" she screamed again.

Kyle began to walk toward the door. His heart skipped a beat and a lump formed in his throat from hearing the apparent pain coming from deep within her. He made it to his office door just as she screamed out his name again. He went for the knob to open it, but stopped himself. Instead, he leaned his back against the door and let out a deep sigh.

"Listen Kyle, I'm not leaving until I see you. I love you Kyle and I don't plan on ever stopping. I know I've made a mistake, but can't you understand that I regret it? I'm not perfect. I'm human just like you, and I'm learning, but I need you to forgive me. Just give me a minute to look you in the eyes, I need that" Zoe paused briefly hoping for a response.

Kyle's body began to feel weak from knowing that he was breaking the heart of the woman who not only loved him, but had once forgiven him and showed him unconditional love when he couldn't find it elsewhere. The truth of the matter was that he was still hurting. He felt like he had to stand firm even if for a little while longer so that Zoe could fully know to never put no one before him and their relationship. As much as it was hurting him and her, he knew it was for the best. He took another deep breath. "Go home, Zoe, or I'll be forced to call security to escort you from the premises."

Zoe couldn't believe what she'd heard. Kyle couldn't be that cold-hearted. Did he no longer love her? She felt her legs give out as she went down on her knees. Once there, she placed her face in the hands of her palms and began to sob uncontrollably. The pain in her heart felt unbearable. She couldn't believe that love was causing her to feel this way again. She tried her best to be a better woman to Kyle than she was to her late husband. The thought of possibly failing again caused her to cry even harder. Why was love constantly playing tricks on her? Was she not good enough to deserve something everlasting? She felt weaker in this moment then she ever had. All of her old demons began to arise, telling her that she wasn't worthy just like she had thought prior. She cried for several minutes more before finally finding the strength in her legs to stand. She took a napkin from her purse and wiped her tear-stained face. She straightened her poster before softly placing her palm flat against Kyle's office door. She closed her eyes and said a silent prayer. She opened her eyes and felt a new sense of strength consuming her. Love, she knew, was powerful and it was also complicated. She'd given up once and refused to a second time. She turned on her heels and began to walk away. She would lose this battle, but she was determined not to lose the war of love.

Chapter Twenty-Three

Cante & Louis

Louis sat on the uncomfortable chair along Cante's bedside. He looked at her normally radiant and vibrant skin and noted how drastically it changed for the worst in a matter of days. She appeared to be losing weight by the minute and her face appeared sunken in as a result. Her body looked extremely fragile and small under the hospital sheets. The sheets did little to cease the chills that were shooting through her body. He held her hand inside his, gently, softly stroking her fingertips which felt like tiny icicles. He just wanted her to always know that someone was there beside her. The erratic beeping from the life support machine that Cante was connected to caused Louis to glance over at it. He hated how the line jumped around in such a volatile way. It caused him both anxiety and grief. He felt like their love was also on the line and he didn't want either to flat line.

He slowly bowed his head into both their hands and began to silently pray. He began to pray for Cante's strength and speedy recovery. He felt the tear that dropped from his eyes land onto her hands. He began to question god, asking him why? Why had the woman that he decided to love come to an unhealthy fate? He questioned god about the timing of it all, they were living their best lives and so happy with one another, so why now?

Louis allowed his emotions to fully show as his tears began to flow freely, he began thinking about their wedding that she'd been planning. It was going to be worthy of being written in history books. He had given Cante the permission to let her imagination run wild with the festivities. He knew that she was planning something out of the ordinary. He remembered how excited Cante had been. Every day, she introduced a new idea to him, disregarding if he agreed with it or not. After a while, he learned how to agree when necessary and to disagree when she wanted him to. His only desire was for her to be happy with the entire arrangement. He wanted this to be the wedding of her dreams, no matter the sacrifice.

Again, Louis began to question God's intentions. How could he have allowed her to become this sick undetected? Why hadn't he given them a sign earlier that could've prevented this all from happening? He felt his body begin to go weak from the thought of possibly losing her. She was truly the air within his lungs, and it all seemed to dissipate when he thought about being without her. He began to gasp for air and his sobs became uncontrollable. He began to pray even harder, giving god his complete faith and control over the situation.

The door to Cante's room opened unexpectedly, causing Louis to look up to see who was entering. Once Louis noticed it was the doctor, he quickly made it to his feet and over to him.

"What's the news, doctor?" asked Louis.

"Let us step outside the room to discuss everything" requested the doctor.

They exited the room. "Okay, now tell me something" demanded Louis impatiently.

"Well, the good news is that it isn't too late. As unfortunate as the situation is, it was just as fortunate that she made it here when she did" said the doctor.

"Please tell me what the illness is" requested Louis.

"Well, the tests have shown that she is suffering from stage four breast cancer" Louis stood unmoving, the implications running wild within his mind.

"So, you said it isn't too late, right?"

"Correct. It's a good thing that we detected it now because we can begin an aggressive form of chemotherapy immediately. If we begin now, her chances for a full recovery improve by eighty percent" informed the doctor.

"Okay, so let's begin" Louis eagerly stated.

"Okay, but there are other matters we need to discuss before we begin" replied the doctor.

"What might those things be?"

"Well…" replied the doctor hesitantly, trying to sound compassionate.

"Well, what?" Spit it out!" demanded Louis more aggressively than he intended.

"Mr. Johnson, this phase of chemotherapy is very expensive. More expensive than Ms Lightfeather's insurance covers" informed the doctor sadly.

Louis went inside his pocket and removed his wallet. Next, he pulled out his Master Card and handed it over to the doctor. "This card has no limit so charge it. Money isn't an issue."

The doctor took the card and examined it. "Okay Mr. Johnson I'll begin processing the paperwork and we'll get her started on her first phase" ended the doctor before turning on his heels and rushing back to his office.

Louis made his way back into Cante's room and over to her bedside. He took her hand into his and again bowed his head and began to silently pray. He needed God's grace now more than ever. He needed Cante to get better for his own sanity. His entire life he believed that his money, expensive cars and mansions were enough to keep him sane; now he knew otherwise. Cante is what now completed him, and he needed God to protect her.

"Please, God" said Louis as he finished praying. He stood up again before kissing Cante's lips. He leaned in and began to whisper into her ear. "Don't worry, baby, you're going to get your wedding no matter what I have to do." Next, he tucked her in before finally the room.

Chapter Twenty-Four

Arnold & Erica

Erica slung open the door to her home and stood in the doorway with an irritated face. She wasn't in the best mood after chasing Arnold Jr. around the house the entire day and was too frustrated to entertain visitors. The breeze that swiftly invaded the doorway did little to cool her mood. She looked out at the woman who was standing before her while holding a toddler in her arm and another little boy who was clamped onto her leg.

"Yes, how may I help you?" asked Erica to the strange woman. The woman appeared to be just as irritated and frustrated as she was. She had a frown upon her almost flawless, fair-skinned face. Her dark hair was tied up in a tight bun and her cat eyes seemed unreal from the way they seemed to change with her movements. Erica had to admit that the woman's beauty was breathtaking.

"Hello, my name is Samantha, and I was hoping to get a few minutes of your time."

"Concerning what?" questioned Erica.

The woman gave Erica a pleading look. "I don't believe this conversation is suitable to be held in a doorway. Could we please come in?"

Erica hesitated briefly before stepping aside and allowing the woman and children inside. She led them to the sitting area and offered them a seat, before asking them if they would like something to drink. The woman declined for the three of them as she shifted her weight on the couch. Erica looked over at the woman and noticed the apparent nervousness within her posture. She figured that something must've really been plaguing the woman's mind.

"Excuse my manners, the name is Erica Simmons" she introduced herself while extending her hand for a handshake.

"Nice to meet you, Ms. Simmons" replied Samantha while shaking Erica's hand. She looked down at the ring on Erica's finger and wondered how it felt to be married.

Erica sat down on the couch adjacent to Samantha and watched as Arnold Jr. came running full speed toward her before jumping into her lap.

"Is he your son?" asked Samantha while staring at Arnold Jr.

"Yes, his name is Arnold Jr. after his father and grandfather" informed Erica proudly before. "I see you have two beautiful children of your own, what are their names?"

"Yes, this is my beautiful daughter Cloe, and this handsome little man right here his name is Blake, I named him after my father" finished Samantha.

An awkward silence took over the area it remained for only seconds before Erica put Arnold Jr. back on his feet.

"Arnold, why don't you go show Blake and Cloe all your new toys inside your playhouse while mommy talks with her friend?"

suggested Erica before looking over at Samantha and asking her if it was okay.

Samantha sat Cloe down and directed the two children to go along with baby Arnold to his playroom. After the kids were gone, another awkward silence filled the room before Erica began to speak.

"Are you sure you wouldn't care for something to drink?" asked Erica again.

"No, thank you" replied Samantha before pausing briefly. "Well, I know you're wondering why I'm here. Before I get to that I'll give you a brief history of who I am. I'm from Chino Hills, California, born and raised. I went to the University of California and graduated with a degree in criminal justice. After college, I began to work as a defense attorney for several years before meeting my boyfriend. I began dating my boyfriend in an off and on relationship before I got pregnant with our son Blake. Things were difficult because his job demanded for him to be gone frequently. I accepted his absence because I loved him and before we knew what had happened, we were pregnant again with our baby girl, Cloe. Now, I know you're wondering why I'm telling you all of this and the reason is because I've been arguing constantly with my boyfriend about not being home enough. I began wondering if he had someone else, so recently while he was asleep, I took the liberty of going through his phone and that's when I came across your name and number."

"Excuse me" replied Erica.

"Yes, I came across your information and, after exploring further, I noticed a large volume of calls and texts between the two of you."

"I think you're mistaken. I'm sorry, Samantha, but I'm certain I don't know who your boyfriend is" informed Erica.

"Erica, my boyfriend's name is Arnold Lamount Simmons."

"Excuse me?" replied Erica with panic in her voice.

Samantha didn't respond she just looked into Erica eyes with pain inside of hers.

"I'm sure there's some confusion here, my husband's name is Arnold Lamount Simmons" informed Erica in confusion.

"That's why I'm here and what I'm here to talk to you about. I found out that my boyfriend has a wife and child that I never knew about."

Erica looked into Samantha's eyes for a sign of deception. She looked deep and could see nothing but pain.

"I don't understand. I don't know how this could be possible. I've been with Arnold for eight years now, we've been married for five and we have a four-year-old child. When did all take place?" asked Erica.

"I met Arnold six years ago while he was in California on business. At the time, he told me that he was in the process of separating from his girlfriend of two years because he believed that she'd been cheating on him. We talked a lot during that time. Eventually, he told me that he was separated and wanted to get exclusive with me. From what I thought we were exclusive and that's when the kids came into play and now…

"I'm here" finished Samantha with agony in her voice.

Erica couldn't believe what she'd just heard. She felt like the world was crashing down around her. She couldn't imagine Arnold committing the actions that were being described to her.

"Your child" began Erica, "the oldest one, how old is he?"

He's five years old…" Erica felt her heart drop to her stomach from the revelation. She'd believed that her child with Arnold was not only her first, but his also. As if Samantha could read her mind, she simply stated that she was sorry. She wasn't sorry about her child but for the lies that Arnold had been telling the both of them. She knew that Erica must've believed her child was his first.

How old is Cloe?" asked Erica without even realizing that a tear had begun to come down her face.

She turns four in about a month," said Samantha as her own tears began to fall.

Samantha understood Erica's pain because it was the same pain that she herself was experiencing. She hated to have to deliver such drastic news, but knew it was imperative to in order for them both to gain some clarity. Her mind had been racing ever since the day she found the messages between Arnold and Erica inside Arnold's phone. After completing her investigation, she knew that she had to meet with Erica to find out the truth.

"I hope you know that I didn't come here with the intention of hurting you. Right now, I'm just as hurt, lost, and confused as you are. Trust me, I was completely oblivious to his manipulation" finished Samantha through tears.

She watched as Erica's tears continued to fall while placing her face inside her hands. Erica slowly lifted her head up and looked sadly into her eyes.

"Samantha, don't take offence to me asking you this, but can I please see some hard evidence?"

Samantha shook her head in agreement before retrieving her purse and reaching inside of it. She pulled out a thick envelope and sat it in front of herself before she began to speak, "The contents of this envelope will most likely hurt you. Again, it isn't my intention to, I need you to understand that we've both been misled here."

Slowly, Samantha handed the envelope over to Erica. Erica looked at the envelope as if it were infected. She hesitated briefly while contemplating on whether or not she should open it. She really wasn't sure if she was prepared to see and accept the contents of the envelope. She was still in a state of denial but knew that she had to face the facts at one point or another. She slipped open the flap of the envelope and began to pull out various amounts of pictures, purchase statements, and two birth certificates. The first things that she examined were the birth certificates. The names on them read Blake Simmons and Cloe Simmons and they were signed by Arnold Lamount Simmons. The next thing she did was pick up all the pictures to examine them. She felt her heart ripping as she viewed pictures of Arnold and Samantha on vacation, professional outings and just lounging around the house. There were pictures of Arnold and the children at playgrounds, birthday parties, and at each of their births. The last pictures were of Arnold, Samantha, and the kids posing for family pictures. As Erica stared down at the pictures, several tears plopped down onto them. There was no more denying it, it was all true.

Erica looked back at the pictures of the two kids and began to see the apparent resemblance between them and Arnold and baby Arnold. It was no denying that the three kids shared the same blood. It was mind boggling to know that Arnold was keeping such a life-changing secret. Erica sat the evidence down and stood up from her stool. She made it over to her liquor cabinet and grabbed ahold of a bottle of Patrón before making her way back over to her seat.

"I guess I'm the one that needs something to drink" she said before giggling to herself. Not bothering to use a glass, she took a gulp directly from the bottle. Feeling the burning sensation in her chest, she grimaced before bringing the bottle back to her mouth and taking another huge gulp.

Samantha opened her mouth to suggest to Erica to slow down but Erica's hand shot up quickly, signaling for her to stop.

"I'm perfectly fine, please do not patronize me" stated Erica before taking yet another surprisingly huge gulp of liquor.

She grimaced again while allowing the liquor to take effect. Both ladies sat opposite one another without exchanging any words. They both were in deep thought about the predicament that Arnold had put them in. "Does Arnold know that you know all of this?" asked Erica after the long silence. Samantha simply shook her head in the negative.

"So, I'm assuming he has no idea about your visit here today, does he?"

"No, he doesn't. He's at my home in Chino Hills and he thinks that I've gone to visit my parents in an emergency. He's waiting there for us to return."

Again, Erica felt a pang in her heart from hearing that Arnold was at her home awaiting them to return while leaving her and their son to feel neglected.

"So, what are you planning to do next?" Erica asked Samantha.

Samantha didn't readily reply as she seemed to be confused, dazed, and lost. Erica might not have realized it, but she was just as hurt as she was. Arnold had given her two children and led her on about one day making her his wife for years. She'd held out hope that eventually they'd become the family that he'd told her they would. Now, she didn't know what to do. "I don't know" she simply stated.

"Samantha, I need some time to figure out what I need to do next as well. I understand that we're both in the same position and that we've both been deceived and betrayed by a man that we love tremendously. I can't tell you how to react next, but woman-to-woman, I'm asking you, for my sake, not to let Arnold know that I know. I just need some time to figure things out. I need time to devise a plan without the distraction of Arnold becoming aware and interfering with my thoughts" finished Erica.

"I understand. You have my word" promised Samantha solemnly.

"I would like to thank you for bringing this to me like a woman. I appreciate the class you've shown throughout this difficult meeting. I understand that you didn't mean any harm and as a woman I too would've handled it similarly. Again, thank you for keeping this between the two of us and know that you must keep faith and strength in the face of adversity" finished Erica, before standing to her feet, letting Samantha know that their visit had come to an end.

Samantha got to her feet before calling out to Blake and Cloe. She gathered them up and thanked Erica for her hospitality. Once they were gone, Erica sat down on the floor and began crying her heart out.

Part 6

Dear Love,

"I gave you my all and you left me with nothing but the taste of salt on my lips from a tear-stained face. You've left me with nothing but a heart that beats loudly and echoes the pain from its broken state. My misery, sorrow, and bitterness are my only company. With you, Love, I once believed that I'd never be lonely. I'd embraced the shivers that you sent through my body from your tender touch. I'd savored the warmth of the arms you used to closely wrap me up. Why did I believe that you were that lone ray of sunlight that peeked through the clouds and misty rain? Why did I have faith in you when you've shown me before that you are nothing but a mirage of such beautiful things? How could you fail me all over again, Love? How could you lead me on then abandon me when I needed you most? You've left me helpless, emotionless, and even motionless, but never again, Love, because here is where it all ends. No longer am I searching for you abroad because through the grace of God I've found true love within!"

-Erica Simmons

Chapter Twenty-Five

Kyle

"So, what you're stating is that you want me to take full control of this account?" asked Alu skeptically.

"Yes, the request isn't one that I'm making. It seems that your hard work has really made a good impression on the guys over at Sulfan. They stated that ever since you've been giving your advice and guidance, that their profit margin has risen at an extraordinary rate. They've given you their full confidence and want only you handling their account" informed Kyle with his most convincing smile.

Alu was ecstatic about this new information that he was receiving. He couldn't believe his luck; this was too good to be true. Ever since Kyle allowed him to begin managing this account, his personal income had increased exponentially. This corporation was making money hand-over-fist and was more than generous with their pay for an accountant of his caliber. The fact that they paid him handsomely was only partially to blame for his newfound fortune. The other part was due to the fact that he was withholding funds and not recording lucrative transactions. This in turn allowed him to pocket healthy sums regularly. He felt like he was in the perfect position, not only did the pharmaceutical company trust him, they trusted him too much.

"So, you're no longer going to be assisting me?" Asked Alu,

"No, it seems like now going to be on your own with this one."

This again excited Alu. He'd been careful with his skimming with Kyle controlling the account with him. He'd managed to stay under the radar without raising any red flags. Now with Kyle out the way, he would really be able to cash in. His palms began to itch from the thought. Now was his opportunity to strike big. Before his handling of this account, he'd been skimming and falsifying reports, allowing him to pocket a cool million here and there to him that was only small gain. He desired wealth. He wanted the kind of wealth that both his business partners possessed. He didn't feel bad about his transgressions because he felt Kyle and Louis were being selfish. While they were flying in private jets, twinkling their toes in million-dollar mansions and doing whatever struck their fancy, he was having a difficult time managing his mortgage payments. He felt that real friends wouldn't be living the highlife while their comrade was struggling to get by. He was only getting his just desserts, he reasoned.

"Thank you so much, Kyle, I'm forever indebted to you" replied Alu with fake gratitude.

"You've worked hard for this opportunity, Alu, and it's about time that all of your hard work starts to pay off. I realize that you've been having a difficult time financially, but those times are now over. You deserve this opportunity and I'm both proud of you and proud to have you on the team. Now, there is just one more thing that I need to discuss with you" announced Kyle.

"What would that be?" asked Alu.

"Well, before I begin, I need you to know that this must remain completely confidential" stated Kyle with a serious tone and expression.

"Yes, of course."

"It hurts me to even relay this but from the information that I've been able to gather I've found out that Louis has been meddling in several of our accounts. It seems that he's been forming shell corporations with which he's been using to launder stolen money from our accounts. He's secretly created his very own falsified ledger and the money that he's been withdrawing has raised red flags within the IRS and SEC. He's now under investigation, but I was forced to pay a fine on behalf of Precise Accounts to clear us of wrongdoing. Alu, trust is hard to find, but I trust you. I need you to help with keeping an eye out for any suspicious activity coming from Louis and alert me once you do."

"Of, course, you know I got your back bro," responded Alu, eagerly.

"It pains me to know that Louis would stoop so low. Money is such a small thing in comparison to friendship…" said Kyle.

"I'm sorry you have to deal with this kind of betrayal, but if it means anything to you, know that you have a loyal friend in me" stated Alu.

"I know, Alu. I know," replied Kyle sadly.

Alu really couldn't believe his luck. This was a perfect circumstance. He understood that red flags would eventually be raised, but never thought that the finger would be pointed at Louis. He knew that he'd been doing a good job with covering his tracks and now it all seemed to be paying off. With Louis being the one in the spotlight, he would use it to his advantage. He would begin to create false accounts and launder even larger sums while making it appear as if the deed was done by Louis. This was indeed going to be a prosperous year.

Kyle walked around his desk and extended his hand out to Alu. Alu grabbed ahold of his hand and shook it vigorously.

"Thanks for your loyalty, Alu. That quality is one that has become rare in today's society. Congratulations again on landing the account" finished Kyle.

"Thank you. I appreciate everything you've done for me. I would hate to end this, but I have a very important obligation to attend to" informed Alu hastily.

"No problem. Business before pleasure" responded Kyle as he watched Alu exit his office.

Once Alu was gone, Kyle sat back down at his desk and loosened his tie. He couldn't believe how conniving Alu was. Not only was he a thief, but he was being a coward by willing to allow someone else to take the blame for his treason. Kyle shook his head in disbelief. He couldn't believe Alu had stooped so low. He knew that Alu had some financial difficulties but had encouraged him that things would get better. He'd allowed his greed along with his lack of patience to get the best of him. Kyle shook his head again before reaching underneath his desk and removing the tape recorder that he had tapped there. He pressed the stop button on it before going deep into thought again. His plan had come together perfectly. After his initial meeting with the representatives of the IRS and SEC he decided to contact his lawyer to set up an additional meeting. The purpose of the second meeting was for them to devise a plan that would help in exposing Alu. They created the Sulfan Pharmaceutical account and allowed the two representatives to pose as the ownership of the company. In the midst of their new investigation, Alu had begun falsifying numerous amounts of reports, not reporting crucial transactions and even giving in favorable advise that led to huge losses. They were also allowing him to overcharge them in service fees all in an effort to incriminate him and ensure a future indictment.

Kyle stood from his desk and began pacing the floor. Again, he shook his head in disbelief before pulling his iPhone from his pocket. He dialed Louis and waited for his answer. Once he had Louis on the line, he began to relay to him all the events of his talk with Alu. Once he finished, Louis only reply was "Checkmate!"

Chapter Twenty-Six

Arnold & Erica

S he said it's your child, and it really messed me up, how could you deny your own flesh and blood, gotta face reality... Mary J. Blige.

Erica sat at her homemade bar sulking in her misery while listening to Mary J. Blige's Your Child and drinking Patron directly from the bottle. On the bar top sat the birth certificates and pictures of Arnold and his kids that Samantha had left her for evidence. Erica was trying her hardest not to cry but was failing the battle badly. She was still in a state of shock, not being able to believe the facts that was presented to her. Arnold had not only committed adultery, but he produced two children while in the act. It all made sense now; his constant trips to California, the receipts that she'd found on occasion of gifts that wasn't for her and the stains she'd noticed on his collars of lipstick that she didn't own. She'd always brushed it off as coincidence. but now it was evident. The revelations hurt badly, but the fact that their child together wasn't his first hurt worst. She couldn't control the tears that began to fall repeatedly as she thought about Arnold's other family. She'd thought that their family was perfect; one to be modeled after but in reality, it all was a mirage. She was now unsure of everything that she thought she knew. Were there any more hidden secrets? Did he really love her? Did he really care about their family?

Erica stood to her feet and began pacing the floor with the bottle of Patron still in hand. She couldn't believe the way Arnold was recklessly breaking his vow's. She knew that she'd once held her own flaws of infidelity in the past but once she said 'I do' none had transpired since. She believed that they'd fixed their issues through counselling and was again faithful and loyal to one another. She'd thought that he'd forgiven her indiscretions now she couldn't help but to think was this all his way of getting retribution for what she'd done to him? As she paced, her legs began to feel like they would give out on her. She couldn't properly describe the pain that she was feeling within, unbearable was an understatement. She sunk to the floor and brought her knees into her before resting her back against the wall of the kitchen. Her tears were now pouring as she allowed her sobs to come from a place deep within her. Her world was shattered. What would she do now? She was afraid of the thought's that were beginning to wander inside her mind. She continued to cry out, trying to release all the pain that was in her soul. She cried until she no longer could. Finally, she made it back to her feet. She decided that she needed to get away from everything and everyone. She needed some time to figure everything out. She took out her phone and called her parents, asking them to keep Arnold Jr. while she went away for a while. After they agreed, she phoned Arnold and told him she would be out of town for a couple of weeks to help aid Cante in an emergency. He told her that it was fine because ironically, he was still in California and wouldn't be home himself for a few weeks.

Chapter Twenty-Seven

Kyle & Zoe

Zoe was stirring constantly in her sleep as she tried unsuccessfully to get comfortable. She flipped over and then turned on her back before flipping over again. Giving up, her eyes finally shot open into the darkness. She awoke to the sound of Mariah Carey's 'We Belong Together' softly playing in the background. She'd forgotten that she'd fallen asleep with the song on repeat as it played throughout her rented condo. She reached over to the other side of her bed in order to wrap her arms around Kyle. She sat up instantly once she remembered that she was in her bed alone instead of in the bed that she shared with Kyle. Loneliness instantly gripped her as the reality of her situation with Kyle set in. She felt more incomplete than she'd ever felt.

Kyle awoke from his sleep with a strong desire to feel the warmth of Zoe's body wrapped in his arms. He turned over to Zoe' side of the bed before reaching to pull her into him. When his arm fell upon the pillow only. It caused him to become fully awake as he sat up in bed. The sound of Lewis Capaidis' 'Someone You Loved' was his only company as it played throughout the house. He'd fallen asleep with the song on repeat while thinking of Zoe. He wiped the sleep from his eyes and allowed them to adjust to the darkness. As he sat alone in bed longing for Zoe, his situation really dawned on him; she was no longer there. The loneliest feeling that he'd ever felt invaded his heart, body and soul; leaving him to feel weaker than he'd ever felt.

* * * * *

Zoe leaned her head back against the soft leather that the headboard was made of and felt the same coldness in it that she felt in her loneliness. She'd been beating herself up constantly about the way she handled things with Kyle and her parents. She'd come to the realization that Kyle was her future husband and that was whose back she should've had. She tried calling him several times, but had received no response. It hurt her badly that he refused to hear her out and made her wonder if he'd ever give her the chance to reconcile. She really missed him. She missed the way that he would cater to her every need. She missed the way he would go out his way to make her happy when she held an attitude and the way he'd get her to laugh when she tried her hardest not to.

* * * * *

Kyle leaned his head back against the massive hardwood headboard and let out an exhausted sigh. He couldn't deny the fact that he really missed Zoe. He also realized that he really needed her as well. He just couldn't seem to overlook the hurt and disappointment that he felt from the way Zoe had handled the situation between him and her parents. He couldn't believe that she'd sided with them when they were the ones in the wrong. Not only that, he was her future husband and the one who she should've supported. He longed to have her back with him. He really missed her. He missed the way that she could make him laugh so easily. He missed the way that she could be so thoughtful and how she'd go to the extreme to surprise him in ordinary ways...

* * * * *

Heartache, Zoe knew, could weigh you down tremendously. She knew that the heartache from a love lost was the worst kind. It did something to her appetite, causing her to not want to eat a thing. She felt light from the weight she lost from the stress. She kicked her feet over the side of the bed before reaching over to the nightstand and retrieving her phone. She pulled up her contact just before coming across Kyle's name...

* * * * *

Pain, Kyle knew, hurt and knew it hurt badly. He knew that the pain caused from love was an excruciating pain. It did something to his body, making him feel weak. He felt exhausted and defeated. He kicked his feet over the side of the bed and went to stand but his legs wouldn't permit it. He reached over to the bedside nightstand to grab hold of his iPhone. He looked at the phone briefly before pulling up his contacts, He got to Zoe's name and stared at it.

* * * * *

Zoe hesitated while looking down at Kyle's name. She wanted so badly to call or text him, but figured that he'd probably continue to ignore her the way that he'd been. She really didn't know what she could do to make the situation better. She still couldn't believe that he'd refused to see her at his office. She really wanted another chance and couldn't imagine being without him. She hated the fact that she'd hurt him and regretted that she'd let him down. She always wanted to be the one person standing beside him when this world ended. She stood from the bed and began pacing the floor. She felt lost and didn't know what was next for her. She quickly lost the strength in her legs to pace as she made her way back to take a seat on the bed. She closed her eyes and began to pray to the one above. She prayed for him to give her the strength to keep fighting for what she loved. She prayed for him to instill inside Kyle the compassion and understanding needed to forgive her. Finally, she prayed that he'd allow Kyle to realize how much she really needed him. She opened her eyes before looking down at her phone and at Kyle's name she pressed her finger into his name, then opened up the text message option. She heard her stomach growl from hunger as she typed her text and sent it. She wished he knew how much she needed her appetite back.

* * * * *

Kyle hesitated while looking down at Zoe's name. Should he call? He contemplated even longer before finally tossing the phone on the bed "Fuck" he cursed to himself. Why did things have to be so complicated? Why couldn't love just be the way that it was meant to be? Why did things have to get so confusing? Why did it always have to hurt? Why did hearts always have to break? All he desired was to truly love and to get true love in return. He didn't want to play the childish mind games, he didn't want to pretend, betray or hurt; he just wanted to love. He laid backward onto the bed and closed his eyes. He began to pray. He prayed for direction and strength. He prayed for a sign that will tell him what he should do with his love for Zoe. He opened his eyes and looked over at his phone before reaching for it. He sat up in his bed and once again looked at Zoe's name. He knew that he was torturing himself by denying himself of her. He pressed his finger into her name and opened up the text message option. The truth of the matter was that he loved her, and he still wanted to be with her. He refused to torture himself any longer. He typed his message and sent it out to her. It was time for him to get his strength back.

* * * * *

The time was two-thirty in the morning when Zoe sent her message and crawled back up inside the bed and got under the covers. She was about to throw her phone back onto the nightstand so that she could wrestle with sleep again but decided to look through some old pictures that she had of Kyle. She began skimming through the pictures and reminisced on the brighter days they'd shared. Man did she really miss him. Her emotions got the best of her as a lone tear slowly trickled down her cheek. She allowed her tears to flow just as her phone began to vibrate inside of her hand, indicating that a text had come through. She couldn't believe her eyes when she noticed that it was from Kyle. She quickly opened it up and began to read, the message simply read…

* * * * *

The time was two-thirty in the morning after Kyle sent his message. He threw his phone back onto the nightstand and crawled up under the covers to his bed. He began to try getting comfortable while thinking about Zoe. He closed his eyes just as his phone began vibrating against the hardwood that the nightstand was made of. He reached over and grabbed it before looking into it. It had the notification that a text message had come through from Zoe. His heart began to beat rapidly as he opened it and began to read. The message simply read... I love you.

Chapter Twenty-Eight

Alu, Kyle, and Louis

Kyle stood tall in his expensive light gray Armani suit holding a glass filled with some of the finest champagne that money could buy. In his company were Alu and Louis, who were there to celebrate the success of the business account that Alu had been put in charge of. Things had planned out perfectly; at least as far as Kyle and Louis were concerned. Alu had been led to believe that the Sulfan Pharmaceutical account was a legit and lucrative account, but what he didn't know was that it was a fictitious account made in order to expose his embezzlement and falsified transactions.

As Kyle stood before them, glass held high and ready to make a toast, he couldn't help but think that all the scamming was coming to an end today. He hated to have to be the one to end Alu's career, but he knew that Alu had brought all of this upon himself; Alu had allowed his greed to get the best of him. Inside, it pained Kyle because he'd been through so much with Alu and he'd considered him a friend, but Kyle understood loyalty was a way of life, not just a word. Kyle held his glass high in the air as he began to address Alu and Louis in a toast.

"First, I would like to say that I'm very proud and thankful to have two very hard working and loyal partners in the two of you. Without y'all, Precise Accounts wouldn't be the successful company that it is today. We've received excellent news regarding the Sulfan account. Thanks to Alu, we've been informed that

Sulfan has not only agreed to extend their contract, but they've also agreed to pay an extra ten percent. The Sulfan account is now our most lucrative account! So, let's toast and give thanks to you, Alu!" finished Kyle deceptively.

Alu couldn't believe what he was hearing as he joined in on the toast. He didn't understand how the owners of Sulfan Pharmaceuticals could be so naïve. He was stealing millions of dollars right from under their noses and still they were eager to continue their business relationship. He had witnessed similar neglect in the past from businesses that weren't keeping proper track of transactions. He'd stolen before and could never understand, how corporations could be so irresponsible. Truthfully, he didn't really care one way or the other. His only concern was to profit from someone else's mistake. He'd went from struggling when he first invested into Precise Accounts to having offshore accounts totaling in the tens of millions; and it was all free money! He smirked to himself when he thought of his good fortune.

Those fools of Sulfan weren't the only ones he was duping, Kyle and Louis were two of the tops in their respective fields and yet, he'd been able to rob them as well. The several fake accounts that he'd created had been allowing him to steal handsomely from Precise Accounts in service fees. He'd been getting paid triple his salary and Kyle and Louis had no idea. He accepted the gesture that Kyle was making on his behalf, he took a healthy gulp of champagne and thought more of his good fortune and of the knowledge that Kyle believed it to be Louis that was responsible for the fraud.

Alu knew he was making it out big and clean. He knew that within days news of the fraud would leak and destroy both Kyle and Louis. Unconsciously, he chuckled to himself thinking about Arnold's brilliant plan. He was killing two birds with one stone and it would effectively give Alu full control of Precise Accounts in its entirety. After the three man gulped their glasses of champagne, Louis stood up and grabbed another bottle of champagne before he announced that he wanted to toast to Alu. He filled all of their glasses again. "I have to admit, at first I was skeptical about embarking upon this venture, I've always believed that you should never mix friendship with business. I've always believed that the two could not remain loyal once intermingled, but I have been proven wrong."

"Thanks to the both of you, I've made money hand over fist and have been fortunate enough to develop and nurture an even stronger friendship with you. This toast is my thanks to you, Kyle, for persuading me to join you in this venture and to you, Alu, for your brilliant mind and ability to lock in such lucrative accounts!" All three man gave a cheer before drowning their glasses of champagne.

Alu looked at Louis and thought to himself *if only you knew.* This was all a game of chess to Alu. He positioned his pieces just the way he needed in order to capitalize his abilities to the maximum. He had to admit that he did truly like both Kyle and Louis but his love for money trumped both loyalty and friendship. In business, there were sharks and there was prey.

"So, Alu," began Kyle, "Is there anything you would like to add before we allow the liquor to fully consume us?"

Alu stood up and smirked at Louis naivete before he began to speak, "I just want to say thank you to the both of you for this opportunity. This is only the beginning of things much greater," He raised his glass in a toast. "To success!"

Glass after glass of champagne was consumed by the three partners. After a while, Kyle got up unsteadily and pushed his way through the double wooden doors of the banquet room and proceeded toward the lobby. He'd been gone for a little longer, then five minutes later he finally returned with two guests. As the three men entered, all Louis and Alu could do was stare, wondering what the purpose of their visit was. Alu stood up and made his way to the two gentlemen with his hand extended for a handshake.

"How are you doing Mr. Jones and Mr. Smith? I did not expect the two of you to be joining us."

"Well, we were invited at the last minute by Mr. Malone. "I suppose he wanted to include us in the festivities since our account is your most lucrative asset."

"Of course." replied Alu.

Louis stood up and made his way over to the gentlemen. He began shaking their hands. "Nice of you two to join us. Allow me to get you two gentlemen a glass of champagne."

The small group of men began sipping their alcoholic beverages and chatting mindlessly on a variety of subjects. After a while, Mr. Jones stood up and began addressing the men.

"I would like to make a toast, if you gentlemen don't mind" he said after receiving their drunken approval he continued.

"Opportunity is the center point of all success. Opportunity is also the cause of much deceit. It was opportunity that led us to Precise Accounts. The opportunity to figure it all out. So, first and foremost, I would like to thank you, Kyle Malone, for your continued cooperation within our business dealings. If it wasn't for you, we would still be slithering in grass filled with snakes! If it wasn't for your corporation, we would still be blinded by false loyalty. Finally, to you, Mr. Francis, it is my pleasure to inform you that you are under arrest for securities fraud, bribery, money laundering and embezzlement."

"What? You've got to be kidding" replied Alu as if he'd just heard a joke.

"No, you heard correctly" responded Kyle while leaning back in his chair and interlacing his fingers behind his head.

"Securities fraud? Money laundering? Embezzlement? I have no knowledge of these accusations" stated Alu deceptively.

Louis cleared his throat before removing the tape recorder from his briefcase. He sat the tape recorder on the desk before pressing play. The room became silent as Alu's voice boomed from the recorder discussing with an unknown male all the fraud that they were committing. After the recording was played, Alu sat down with a shocked expression on his face.

"How do you know that's my voice on that recording? That could be anyone."

"There's video surveillance that accompanies the recordings, Mr. Francis. Would you like for me to show you them as well or would you like the chance to discuss all of this with your lawyer before you further incriminate yourself" stated the heavyset representative.

With that option, Alu stood up and placed his hands behind his back! The representative approached him and began to handcuff and mirandize him. Alu had his head down as they walked him toward the exit. Before they exited, they stopped and again thanked Kyle and Louis for their help. Once the men were gone, Kyle addressed Louis. "I didn't want to say this in front of the two representatives, but I know who Alu's co-conspirator who was on them tapes with him. I can never forget that voice."

"Who?" asked Louis eagerly.

Kyle paused briefly as he thought about Arnold and of their last encounter. He had a feeling that he would cross paths with Arnold again one day, but hadn't imagined that it would be in the manner that he was planning.

Chapter Twenty-Nine

Arnold & Erica

Erica walked slowly down the dirt-filled trails of the park. The wind blew lightly but steady as the leaves on the trees went with its flow. She inhaled deeply to allow the fresh air to fill her lungs and give her mind and body a different energy. She took in the scents of the air and it reminded her of why she loved the fall season so much. The sound of a decaying, dark green, dark brown and burnt orange leaf crushing under her boot brought her thoughts away from the scenery and back to the chaos that enveloped her world. She'd been lost and confused among other things and had realized that she needed to find herself before it was too late. Her thoughts terrified her because her fragility made her feel like ending it all. She knew that she had to find strength; not for herself but for her son. She'd talked to him often but only by phone. The innocence in his voice as he asked of not only her whereabouts, but of the whereabouts of his father had left a hurtful pain in her heart. What could she tell him? That his father was no good? That he manipulated her, deceived her and that he was a liar and a cheater? Could she tell him that because of the pain and hurt she was feeling, as a result of his own father's betrayal, that she couldn't stand to be around anyone... Not even him.

Of course, she couldn't, no matter how much she despised Arnold at the moment she couldn't imagine painting those images of him inside of their child's mind. She refused to let their child know just how shattered his father had left her. Instead, she gave him the excuse that she asked her parents to corroborate which was that they were both off on important business trips. She thought about her parents and how they'd offered her their support without a second thought. She remembered the look of compassion and sorrow that her mother gave her after hearing the transgressions of Arnold.

She also remembered the look of complete anger and insanity that her father had from the knowledge that the man he had given his blessings to take care of his daughter had failed not only him but her, tremendously. After leaving Arnold Jr. in their care, she made her way out of town and away from everything and everyone. She was finding a bit of solace, if not peace. The first week was the hardest: long days lying in bed under her covers crying until her eyes were puffy feeling her body lose weight from lack of eating. She had to force herself to get down half her portions of food only to allow the thoughts of Arnold and his second family to send it coming right back up again. She could smell her own body odor throughout the room in that time, it wasn't a pleasant one, rather one that showed she hadn't made it from her bed to the shower in quite some time. Yes, that week was the hardest and the fact that she had turned off her phone to tune out the world didn't help much either, leaving her to tend to her depression all alone.

In that time, she felt that she'd go insane, the visions of Arnold with another woman, with other kids, with another family plagued her thoughts constantly and brought her down levels lower than the depths of the sea. It had taken her a week to get out of bed, to eat an entire meal and to begin showering regularly. Since then, she had turned her mobile device back on, ignoring all of the voice messages and text messages left not only by Arnold, but Cante and her mother as well. The one person she did talk to was her father. She had been talking to him constantly and regularly. He did more listening than talking, but when he did talk, she felt the compassion and love within his words and advice.

He'd offered her perspectives that she accepted and at times rejected but in which she knew were correct. To him, there was no excuse for what Arnold had done. He knew that his daughter didn't deserve that type of treatment; no one did. He also knew that love and marriage weren't easy commitments to be involved in. He knew those struggles firsthand and could remember his union with her mother almost succumbing to those very struggles. No, their problems weren't as extreme as what she and Arnold faced, but they were problems nonetheless. To him, one betrayal was no worse than another, no lie was worse than the other and no sin was worse than another. With that understanding, he was able to not only help her but make her look deep within herself. He had to remind her of her past and ask her at one point was she any better than Arnold? No, she didn't have kids with another man, but she had lain in the arms of another man.

She had once deceived Arnold, betrayed him and professed her love to someone else when he was being totally faithful to her. She had at one point brought him to his knees and caused him to almost take a life for her love, was his betrayal of her any worse than her betrayal of him? It was those conversations with her father that now consumed her thoughts and is what gave her the strength, empathy, and clarity that she needed. The wind began to pick up and the leaves seemed to fight against its force in order to stay attached to their branches. Erica fastened her peacoat tighter and pulled down her wool beanie over her ears.

She made her way over to a bench that sat off to the side of the trail and she sat down while she continued to reflect on her life. She had to admit to herself that she still loved Arnold dearly and even more than that, she was still in love with him deeply. She understood that no one was prefect and as he had tried at one point, he was still no exception to that rule.

She missed him. There was no doubt about that, but she didn't know if she could forgive him and accept the children that he had had out of wedlock. He had broken his vows to remain true and faithful to her. He let her and their child down when they had depended on him. These thoughts hurt her but the thought of her giving up on their marriage hurt her equally. What would she tell her son? How could she live life separately from him when their life had become all she knew? She reflected on her vows to him; through sickness and health, for better or for worse...

Wasn't this for worse? Would she be no better than him if she walked away? Ending the promise, she not only made to him but that she made before god as well. That thought put her in a trance and alone tear trickled slowly down her cheek. She understood struggle and had never been one to quit easily or forget. However, she also wasn't one to allow herself to be mistreated. She deserved better, Arnold Jr. deserved better, their family deserved better she concluded. It was time for her and Arnold to meet face-to-face and address these issues. She slowly rose from the bench and began walking back to her cabin. She was being forced to make a tough decision; was what they had built together worth abandoning?

Chapter Thirty

Arnold

The darkened alleyway reeked of urine, smoke, and trash, amongst other things. The sounds of highly intoxicated bums arguing and police sirens wailing sounded as Arnold anxiously paced back and forth in the darkness. He quietly cursed Alu for choosing such a shady destination to conduct their business in. He looked at his watch to check the time again as his patience wore thin with Alu's tardiness. He'd rushed to their designated meeting spot after receiving a 911 text from Alu demanding that they speak immediately. He had a feeling that something must've gone horribly wrong, and it worried him. He unconsciously reached inside his waistband to feel the weight and cold steel of his Colt forty-five pistol that he had concealed there. He didn't have time for any mishaps and began to get the feeling that Alu had made a huge mistake. If that was the case, he planned on covering his tracks by leaving Alu slumped in the alleyway like one of the drunken bums, if necessary. He refused to get implicated in a conspiracy that could ultimately not only end his career, but land him in prison as well. He tensed up as he heard a car pull up from behind him before killing its lights. The tint on the windows allowed for the occupant's identity to be concealed. Arnold walked toward the car just as the door opened and the man began to exit.

"What the hell took you so long? I've been waiting for over an hour" fussed Arnold before the man could fully exit the vehicle.

"I got here as fast as I could," replied the man, once he realized that the man wasn't Alu, but Kyle. "What the fuck are you doing here?"

"You don't sound too happy to see me," jested Kyle with a smirk on his face.

"You have two seconds to tell me what you're doing here or..."

"Or what?" asked Kyle as he interrupted Arnold. Arnold began reaching into his waistband to grab ahold of his pistol.

"I wouldn't do that if I was you," said a voice from behind Arnold.

Arnold turned around and was face-to-face with Louis who was aiming a forty-caliber handgun directly at him. Arnold froze.

"You have two seconds to put your hands where I can see them, or I'll be forced to pump a few of these shells into you" warned Louis.

Arnold did not contest as he put his hands in the air. He could see the seriousness in Louis' face and did not want to risk testing him. Kyle walked up to Arnold and removed the handgun from his waistband before standing in front of him.

"I see some things never change" stated Kyle, referring to Arnold's gun that he held to his hand.

"What the fuck do y'all want?" asked Arnold while refusing to appear shaken.

"I think you know exactly what we're here for. I'm sorry to be the one to inform you, but your associate Mr. Francis is now in federal custody as we speak" informed Kyle.

"I have no idea what you are talking about" replied Arnold.

"Come on now, Arnold, you know exactly what we're talking about" replied Louis while adjusting his grip on the gun.

"So, you here to do a citizen's arrest?" asked Arnold in a joking manner as he laughed to himself.

"Naw" replied Kyle. "We're here to let you know that we are more than aware of your bullshit. Did you really believe that you would be able to bring us down with a corruption plot?"

"Again, I don't know what you're talking about" responded Arnold with a smirk on his face.

Kyle approached Arnold and stood toe-to-toe with him.

"If I were you, I would back up just a little. You remember what happened to you the last time we stood toe-to-toe" warned Arnold.

"If it's up to me, this time will have a very different outcome" threatened Louis as he walked closer to Arnold with his gun turned on him.

Arnold looked back toward Louis with contempt in his eyes as he quietly wished that he hadn't gotten caught slipping. If he had still had his gun in his possession, shots would have already been fired.

"Again, I ask what the fuck do y'all want?"

"Again, we just came her to inform you that the gig is up. Your little scam didn't work. I don't know how someone with such a small IQ as you could believe you would outsmart us. You can't think long-term enough and your money isn't long enough to cripple us. Also, I never had the chance to let you know how good it felt to be in between the legs of your woman while you were lying at home wondering where she was. It was indeed incredible" taunted Kyle.

"You motherfucker! I will kill your ass" replied Arnold as he aggressively stepped towards Kyle.

The sounding of the forty-caliber pistol firing caused Arnold to stagger backwards in shock. He frantically felt his body all over to feel for any holes that might be in him.

"If you move again, the next shots won't be in the air, they will be in your forehead. Now, test me to see whether or not I'm bluffing" warned Louis as he gripped the pistol even tighter.

"You just couldn't leave well enough alone, huh? I was able to look past the fact that you shot me only because I knew that I was wrong. I stayed away from you and your wife, but still you try to destroy me. Just so you know, you'll never be man enough to destroy someone of my character. I'm here warning you to never try again because if we have to ever cross paths again, one of us, will end up in a casket and I guarantee you it won't be me" finished Kyle before taking a step back from Arnold.

"Are we done here yet?" asked Arnold while still exuding bravado.

"No, there's one more thing" replied Kyle as he cocked back and punched Arnold square in the jaw. Arnold fell to the ground instantly.

"I've been wanting to do that for years," said Kyle. "We are done here" he finished as he, along with Louis, hopped back into their vehicles and pulled away from the darkened alleyway leaving Arnold laying disoriented with blood slowly trickling from his mouth.

Chapter Thirty-One

Cante & Louis

Louis sat inside a café in downtown Chicago sipping a French vanilla cappuccino while reading the Chicago Tribune. He skimmed through the business section, looking for any notable news. He looked to see what was happening on Wall Street. He noticed some blue-chip stocks that took hits due to the impending trade war with China. He not only held stock in companies in a variety of indexes, but he owned companies offered on both the Dow and S+P 500. After reviewing the indexes, he began browsing the local news. In the process, his mind began to wander. He began to think about Cante and her upcoming release from the hospital. He was all set to pick her up tomorrow and had planned to surprise her with something special. A smile formed on his face from just the thought of it. He couldn't wait to see Cante's reaction to what he had planned for her. He knew that he needed to make her feel secure and confident again. She had been self-conscious of her appearance following the chemotherapy she had to endure, and she had begun doubting whether or not Louis viewed her the same as a result of her transformation. He hated not only what she was enduring physically but what she had been going through mentally. He loved her regardless.

"Louis, is that you?!" Louis was instantly snapped away from his thoughts after hearing his name called. He looked up and noticed the dark chocolate complected woman addressing him. She had her long, black hair laying straight down her back. Her thick, luscious lips were turned up into a smile and her hand rested on her thick thigh that was squeezed tightly into a light-gray business skirt. Her perfectly proportioned breasts stood out in her long-sleeve white blouse. Louis looked into her hazel eyes and he instantly recognized her.

"Sylvia" he said while getting to his feet," long time no see," he said while reaching to embrace her. She fell into his arms and wrapped her arms around his waist. His cologne was intoxicating to her and her perfume had the same alluring effect on him. They separated and again they began examining one another. After their eyes were satisfied with what they were absorbing, Louis offered Sylvia a seat. She sat down adjacent to him as they began to talk.

"What are you doing back in Chicago? If I recall correctly, I thought you had moved to Atlanta" inquired Louis.

"Yes, I'm still residing in Atlanta. I'm here promoting my new makeup line" she replied.

"Still all business, huh?" asked Louis.

"Hell, I should be saying that to you. You were always out of the country on one business trip or another. I'm surprised you are not in China or Japan right now" she joked.

"Guilty" replied Louis.

"Well, I see you haven't changed, you are still as handsome as I remember" complimented Sylvia.

"And you are still as sexy as I remember" replied Louis.

"If I was so sexy, why'd you stop calling?" she asked.

It had been several years since Louis had seen or talked to Sylvia. They had been a thing for about three weeks, which at the time was the longest time Louis had consistently spent with one woman. He really had been enjoying Sylvia. She was intellectual funny, sexy, and fun. Not to mention that the sex was the bomb.

"I guess life happened" he told her.

"I tried calling you several times. I Facebooked you and even stopped by your office on more than one occasion. I just gave up when I started feeling like some kind of stalker." Sylvia sadly replied.

"I apologize for that. It wasn't anything against you. Trust me when I say that, I really had been enjoying your company…. But like I said, life happened" he said.

"What does that mean?" she asked him.

Louis contemplated this question. When he said life happened, what he really meant was that Cante happened. It was when he went to Minnesota and met Cante that he decided to end his rendezvous with Sylvia. Sylvia was breathtakingly beautiful, but Cante literally had stolen the air right out of his lungs. He had felt bad about how he went about avoiding Sylvia, but he felt they had run their course and that a new chapter in his book was being written. He knew that she'd been catching feelings for him and he had to admit that he felt something for her as well.

"A variety of situations that I would rather not discuss right now" stated Louis.

"I understand. Well, the past is the past. We're here in the present and I must admit, when you hugged me, your cologne did something to the tender place in between my legs," teased Sylvia.

"Still right to the point, huh?" he asked.

"Aren't you the one that once told me that is the only way to be?" she replied.

"Guilty again. I have to admit that your beauty has always done something to me" Louis said.

"Tell me about it" replied Sylvia.

Louis stared into her eyes. She licked her lips seductively as she stared back intensely. He had to admit she still had some kind of power over him. She wasn't only crazy fun, but she was crazy in the bedroom.

"I'm waiting" said Sylvia as she lifted her leg underneath the table and sat her feet into Louis' lap gently, she allowed her foot to caress his manhood. Louis hissed in ecstasy. He began feeling himself becoming extremely aroused. Sylvia had mastered the art of seduction and knew exactly how to put a man under her spell when needed. Louis closed his eyes as she continued rubbing his long shaft with her foot. He felt himself losing control before he quickly regained it. His eyes shot open as he slid his chair back, causing Sylvia's foot to slip from his crotch.

"What's wrong?" she asked, surprised. Louis quickly stood up and straightened his attire. He took hold of his briefcase as Sylvia rose to her feet.

"I'm sorry, Sylvia. As much as I would like to take you into the bathroom and fuck the shit out of you until you are screaming at the top of your lungs, I just can't. We had so much fun back then and I will forever remember those times but I'm at a different place in my life now. I'm engaged to be married to a beautiful woman who owns my heart and my loyalty. Sorry, again…."

finished Louis as he quickly brushed past her and made it outside to his car.

Once inside, he leaned his head back and inhaled deeply. Temptation, he knew, was a motherfucker. He loved Cante and refused to allow a temporary satisfaction to end something everlasting. He setup straight once again regaining his composure. He started his ignition and allowed WGCI radio station to fill the speakers. Louis chuckled to himself once he realized that Dave Hollister's 'One Woman Man' was playing. *How ironic* he thought to himself as he merged with traffic on Lakeshore Drive. He had a long day ahead of him in preparation for the surprise he had in store for Cante.

Chapter Thirty-Two

Cante & Louis

Ed Sheeran's 'Thinking Out Loud' was playing… I'm thinking people fall in love in mysterious ways, maybe just like the touch of a hand…

The day that Cante was released from the hospital, Louis made sure he was there to take her home. It had been nine months of repeated chemo sessions, injected medicines and declines of health but now the cancer was in remission. Cante felt stronger than she had in a while, but she also felt self-conscious. To her, she was not her normal, beautiful self. She struggled with the reality of her mastectomy and the reality of her chemo-induced baldness. The day of her release, she stood in her hospital room's bathroom staring into the mirror. Tears began to well up in her eyes as she examined herself. She couldn't believe the drastic changes the disease had exacted on her body. Along with the loss of her breasts and her hair, she had lost a drastic amount of weight. She didn't know how to feel as she touched the parts of her body that had changed dramatically. She ran her hand over a head and used the other hand over her bare chest.

She knew that her hair would eventually grow back, and she was thankful that she'd been given a second chance at life, she just didn't know if Louis would still feel the same way about her with the changes. Would he still love her if she weren't able to go back to normal? Will he still be supportive if the cancer recurred its ugly face again? Would he still want to marry her knowing the vitality of all these circumstances surrounding her?

Louis had sat by her bedside day in and day out. There were times when he would only leave her to shower and sleep in anything but a chair. He helped her dress, eat and bathe when she was weak to do so herself. He would read her stories well into the night, even after she had already fallen asleep. Oftentimes, he would spend hours talking to her all the while thinking she was asleep. She would lay there awake, unbeknownst to him, just listening to him tell his deepest fears. She listened to him talk about his childhood. He talked about his past as a playboy in college and early professional life. She listened as he reminisced on the day that they had first met. They had met at a club and what he recounted as the best sex of his life. He spoke of the fear he had had when he began to realize that he was beginning to have feelings for her. She'd heard him say how scared he was when he realized that he had actually fallen in love with her. He didn't know how many times she heard him cry while holding her hands within his, praying for God not to take his soulmate away from him.

She tried her hardest not to cry with him as she lie there pretending to be asleep instead, she'd prayed for the strength to not only get her through this but to get them through it all. She'd told herself to be strong and to fight for their future. Now as she stood in the mirror with tears streaming down her face, she again began to pray. She prayed that he would still love her through it all. She quickly began to wipe away her tears as she heard the door to the hospital room open and then close. She heard Louis call out to her before she walked out of the bathroom. She watched as a wide smile spread across his face the moment he saw her. His smile automatically made her do the same in return.

"Hey, my beautiful queen, I see that you are up and ready to blow this hot dog stand" he said as he walked over to her. Self-consciously, she looked down at her emaciated body before quickly looking back into his eyes. She watched as he walked up on her and braced herself as he embraced her in a tight hug. She felt small in his arms and wondered to herself, did he feel the difference in her body? She feebly hugged him back and felt it as his cheek rested along her bald head. She wondered, did he regret not being able to inhale the smell of her long hair? A part of her wanted to separate herself from his embrace when she felt her bare chest pressed up against his tight stomach. Slowly, he released her and stepped back with his hands resting on her shoulders and gazed into her eyes.

"What's the matter?" he asked of the sad look she was giving him.

"Nothing," she replied.

"You know I know better" he replied. "Talk to me."

Cante looked down at the floor in order to avoid making eye contact. She felt it as the tears began to well up in her eyes. She did her best not to cry as she vulnerably said "Look at me, Louis."

"I am looking at you" he replied, confused.

"No, I mean really look at me. Don't you recognize that my head is bald, that I have lost a lot of weight and that my breasts are gone? Louis, I feel hideous!" she exclaimed as tears began to fall.

The sight of her crying nearly broke Louis' heart. He took his hand and tilted her head up so that she could look him in the eyes.

"Cante, you are and always will be to me the most beautiful woman that has ever walked this earth. When I look at you, I can't help but to feel like a little boy with a childhood crush. My knees still get weak every time I look into your eyes and my heart gets this indescribable feeling when I see you smile."

"But look at me, Louis, how could you feel that way when I've changed?"

"Because I can't help it, Cante. I can't help the effect that you have on me or the way that I feel about you. There's nothing in this world that could make me feel differently. I love you with everything I have, and I accept you in every way that you are. You are my queen, Cante."

"But what if I don't get back to normal? What if the cancer returns worse than before?" Cante looked into Louis' eyes and felt more self-conscious, weak and vulnerable in those few seconds than she had her entire life.

"You might not even be sure that you still want to marry me" she finished as she watched him take a few steps back from her. He began to stare at her harder, glaring as if he was really seeing her for the first time.

"You're right," he finally said as he began to walk away from her. She watched him as he walked toward the door and retrieved his overcoat that he had splayed out on the hospital room couch. The tears really started to come as her insecurities were confirmed. Why would he want someone that has diseased cells when he could have any healthy women in the world?

"I knew it" she softly whispered to herself as her heart felt like it was slowly breaking. She watched Louis head toward the door before slowly stopping. He turned on his heels suddenly and began to walk back toward her.

Once he was in front of her, he reached into his blazer pocket before saying, "I'm positive that I still want to marry you."

Next, he pulled out a black velvet box and dropped down on one knee. "Cante" he began, "we've been through so much over these last months, but we're still standing. I prayed that we would make it through, and we have. Cante, I love you so much and I will forever love you no matter what physical changes that you go through. I couldn't possibly live without you being in my life" he paused briefly before opening up the jewelry box so that Cante could see that twenty carat diamond wedding ring inside.

"Cante, I'm right here in front of you on one knee again because I need you to know that I loved you before cancer, through cancer, and ill love you the same if, God forbid, it comes back. With that being said, Cante I would like to know, will you marry me?"

Cante looked down on Louis and felt her knees go weak, before she knew it she had fallen to her knees and quickly hugged Louis around the neck her tears were uncontrollable as she told him "yes" over and over again. They sat on the hospital floor holding one another for what seemed like an eternity. Finally, Louis separated them. He used his hands to wipe away her tears before kissing her passionately on the lips. Next, he brought his lips to her ear before whispering, "You know the good thing about all of this?" he asked.

"What?" Cante asked softly.

"Now you'll able to get those DD implants that you've always wanted" Louis said jokingly.

"Louis!" exclaimed Cante as they both let out a much needed laugh.

Chapter Thirty-Three

Kyle pulled his peacoat tighter across his body and ducked his head low while trying to prevent being blown away by the vicious winds that were ripping through the streets of Chicago. He only had a few paces to go before he was safely inside Big Momma's domain, but the whipping winds made it seem much longer. Normally, Kyle wouldn't have subjected himself to the assault of this kind of weather, but he'd come running when Big Momma called. Once inside he began clicking his Timberlands boots against one another to rid them of the snow. The heat that was circulating throughout the house gave it a welcoming feel. He began to call out to Big

Momma while walking through the house. After receiving no response, he made his way toward the kitchen. He could smell the wafting aromas of her soul food and felt his stomach growl instantly.

Once inside the kitchen, he noticed she wasn't there but several of her finished dishes were. Quietly, he crept over the counter, he looked back over his shoulder quickly before using his finger to sample some of the banana pudding. He closed his eyes and savored the shock it had on his taste buds. Next, he took a spoon from the counter and smoothed over the crime scene. He called out to Big Momma again before heading toward the living room. Once there, he noticed Big Momma sitting on the couch with her back toward him. She was joined by a visitor who also had their back to him. They sat closely as they appeared to be examining something. Big Momma must've felt his presence. "How was the banana pudding?" she asked.

Caught off guard, his only reply was, "HUH?"

Big Momma chuckled to herself. "Get on in here Chilli," Kyle shook his head in astonishment wondering how she was always able to figure him out so easily. He finally made it around the couch but stopped in his tracks after seeing who Big Momma's guest was. His heart began to flutter and the butterflies floated gracefully around in his stomach.

"Don't just stand there looking as if you've seen a ghost, Chilli, take a seat," commanded Big Momma without looking up from the photo album that she had on display. Kyle took a seat on the love seat adjacent to them and tried to maintain his composure. He watched Big Momma point to a picture. "That's Kyle on his first day of kindergarten, that child's head was bigger than his body" Big Momma chuckled briefly. "Just look at that smile, It brightened the room, missing tooth and all" she finished in admiration.

Zoe couldn't help but to laugh as she looked at the picture. She kept her eyes glued to the photo album because she was afraid to look up into Kyle's eyes. Big Momma took the time to point out several more embarrassing childhood photos of Kyle as he sat across from them with his heart racing faster than his mind. Big Momma placed the photo album on the dining room table. She looked over at Kyle.

"Chilli, I can still remember the very first time I introduced your poppa to my mother and father. Your grandmother was in awe of that chocolate, well-built handsome young man who I talked her ear off about. Your grandpa, however, was an entirely different story. To him, no man deserved me or was good enough for me. To him, I was just too young, immature, and not ready to be in love. He was a stubborn man that was hard to convince. He forbade me from seeing your poppa right on the spot. He said that I didn't know What love was and that if I thought I was grown enough to beg to differ, then I was a longer allowed under his roof. I was 16 years old, and I knew what I was feeling in my heart. I knew that I wanted to be with your papa no matter what consequences came from it. My father gave me an ultimatum and I didn't even have to make the choice because your papa grabbed me by the hand and led me away. Once we got alone, he told me that I didn't have to worry about a thing because he would take care of me. After that, I didn't speak to my father for years even though I tried time and time again. Eventually, my father realized he couldn't control faith and in the end he warmed up to the inevitable. Chilli, the point I'm trying to make is that there's always going to be outside forces that try to pull you apart. It's just the world we live in but you have to stick together during those times. In a relationship all you have is one another when it's all said and done, yes, you could love other people, but you can't allow other people's views, opinions, or suggestions to interfere into or dictate your relationship" Big Momma paused briefly before looking over at Zoe.

"Chilli, your parents are people with their own beliefs. Believes that you obviously don't share. Your parents are also two people that have one another. If you were alone, you're alone but as you sit here right now they still are together. You have a life of your own to live, a love of your own to give and a family of your own to build. Don't end up being alone forever trying to please the unpleasable."

She looked from Zoe to Kyle before slowly lifting herself from the sofa, and began wobbling her way toward the kitchen before saying, "Let me go check on this cornbread, Chilli, I sure don't want to burn it."

She excused herself to leave Kyle and Zoe to face one another. Silence dominated the space between them as they set awkwardly across from one another trying to avoid eye contact. Finally, Zoe glanced over at Kyle and he looked into her eyes. They stared at one another while trying to muster up enough courage to speak.

After a moment Zoe addressed him. "Kyle I'm sorry for the way I handled the situation with my parents. It was really inconsiderate of me to not take into account your feelings. Also, I should've forewarned you of my parents' views and I should've had your back against them. I'm so sorry if you feel like I left you stranded, and I want you to know that I'll never put you in a position to have to feel like that again."

Kyle didn't reply as he took in her words. He'd felt let down by Zoe and felt like she didn't stand ground for him properly. Slowly, Zoe got up and made her way over to him. She gently nudged herself alongside him in the small loveseat. She looked him in the eyes again.

"Kyle, I understand that I still have a lot of learning to do. I haven't figured out the right way to go about most things. I still have a lot of mistakes to make but I'm willing to learn and I'm willing to learn from my mistakes. Yes, I love my parents, but I love you as well. My parents can't give me what I need, only you can do that, it took this situation for me to see that when the dust settles it's just us, not us and them" she paused letting her words take effect.

"Kyle, I need you and only you. I need you to correct me when I'm wrong, to pick me up when I fall, to be my strength when I'm weak. Most importantly, I need you to continue to love me even when it's hardest to" Zoe finished just before a tear escaped her eyes.

Kyle took his hand and gently wiped it away. He could see the remorse and compassion seeping from within her eyes. There was no doubt that he loved her. He knew that what they had was real and felt their connection in his soul. He realized that no situation nor person was perfect. The moment he'd given Zoe his heart was the moment he accepted her; flaws and all. Without any words, he leaned in and kissed Zoe upon the lips. She grabbed hold of him and hugged him tightly. She'd felt lost without him and couldn't imagine living her life that way. What she desired was true love. A real, genuine, authentic love. She knew that what she had with Kyle was all these things and more. She held him tighter as she closed her eyes and thanked the lord for his many blessings. Once she opened her eyes, she saw Big Momma standing off in the distance, watching them, with a smile on her face.

Chapter Thirty-Four

Arnold made his way inside the house and grudgingly loosened his tie before discarding his jacket on the coat rack. Next, he began to call out to Erica. After getting no response, he made his way through the house, continuing to call out to her. He made his way into the dining area and he finally found her, the sight of her caused him to be instantly aroused. She stood almost completely naked aside from her bra that accentuated her breasts and a tiny thong that did little in the way of hiding her plump ass and thick legs. In her hand was a glass filled with wine that she sipped seductively.

"Welcome home, honey" she enticingly greeted. The red wine gave her lips a sultry and lethal appeal. Her lips twisted into a sneer that she instantly transformed into a smile. She made her way around the table that was filled with his favorite foods and candlelight. "Where's my son?" asked Arnold tiredly.

"I dropped him off at my parents. I wanted us to have this evening all to ourselves" replied Erica. "Let me make you comfortable, husband, I'm sure you're hungry and you look exhausted."

Arnold watched as Erica approached. She sat her wineglass on the table before walking behind him and bringing her hands up to his shoulders. Slowly, she began messaging all the tension that she felt inside of them. Arnold closed his eyes, reveling in the moment and Erica's magical hands.

"So, how have you been?" Erica asked after sitting Arnold down into a chair at the table, continuing to massage his shoulders, head, and neck.

"Good" he responded.

"Relax, baby" stated Erica. "Let me make our plates so that we can talk and enjoy this delightful meal" said Erica as she proceeded to fill their plates with food. After setting Arnold's plate down in front of him, she made her way to her seat.

Arnold watched his wife in awe. She looked extremely alluring and it made his loins stir. He tried controlling himself while simultaneously stuffing his mouth with food. He didn't know what possessed her to surprise him this evening but, whatever the reason, he was grateful for it. There wasn't too much he enjoyed more than Erica's cooking, he complimented her on her cooking skills constantly so when he looked up and noticed Erica hadn't touched her food, it caused him to ask her what the matter was.

"Nothing" lied Erica. "I'm just getting more satisfaction from watching you enjoy your meal." Arnold allowed Erica's words to play in his mind, he began to tell her that she was acting a bit suspiciously but opted not to, not wanting to kill the mood she'd created. He tried breaking the ice by asking her more. "How have things been?"

"Things have been really eventful" replied Erica with a hint of incense in her voice. Arnold caught the apparent change of tone. He looked over at his wife with a confused look. He never knew her to speak in riddles and could tell something was up with her. "And what is that supposed to mean?" asked Arnold finally.

"I'm sorry, honey, for my tone and choice of words. I just momentarily allowed myself to think back on a conversation I had and it upset me all over again" she relayed.

"What conversation was that?" asked Arnold.

Erica didn't reply right away. She took the time to pick up her fork and stuff a couple of pieces of shrimp inside her mouth. She allowed the food to prevent her from saying the things that she really wanted to say. Was he really sitting in front of her pretending like he didn't have an entire family on the side? The thought almost made Erica regurgitate. Still, she gave Arnold her most convincing smile. "Let's not allow that to spoil the mood" she said before getting up and making her way back over toward Arnold. She began to gently run her hands over his bald head in a gentle caress.

"Don't allow my problems to worry you, baby. This moment is all about you, my king, and your relaxation" said Erica while she continued to massage Arnold's head. Next, she quickly whipped her legs across Arnold's lap, sitting firmly against his hardened manhood and simultaneously grinding against him. The feeling caused Arnold to hiss and his hands instantly gripped Erica's ass.

"Slow down just a little bit, handsome, the night is still young" stated Erica before lifting herself from his lap. "Let me feed and cater to you," stated Erica before grabbing Arnold's steak knife and his fork and began expertly cutting his steak into bite-sized cubes. Slowly, she began feeding Arnold. The steak was so tasty that it caused Arnold to close his eyes as he savored it. He sat both his hands flat on top of the table as a sense of complete relaxation swept over him while Erica fed him.

"How is it, baby?" asked Erica.

"There's nothing better than your steak" replied Arnold as he savored it.

"Yeah" replied Erica with a devilish smirk on her face. She tightly gripped the knife that she was using to feed Arnold. Quickly, she brought the knife up and then down into Arnold's hand that rested against the table, nailing it to the spot.

"Ahhhhh!!" yelled Arnold at the shock of the pain searing red-hot through his hand. "What the fuck?!" he screamed while trying to pull the knife free with his other hand. Erica grabbed hold of his free hand, effectively preventing him from pulling the knife away. Erica began laughing and the look on her face was one of complete and utter insanity.

"There's no use in screaming, honey. No one will hear it... does it hurt?" she taunted.

"Erica... Erica... Please..." panted Arnold in pain.

"Yeah, I'm sure it hurts, but at least the knife is only in your hand. Trust me, it hurts much more to be stabbed in the back" replied Erica, letting Arnold know that she was aware of his betrayal.

"Erica, please remove the knife... Please... Erica, I'm not sure what it is you think you know... or heard... but, if you give me a chance... I'm sure I could clear up any confusion..." pleaded Arnold.

"No, there isn't any confusion. I'm one hundred percent certain in what I know of you, Samantha, and the kids" Erica finished causing Arnold's entire body to lose strength. How did she know about that?

"You're wondering how I know about them, aren't you?" asked Erica rhetorically. Slowly, she removed Arnold's tie from around his neck before using it to bind his free hand to the chair. His blood ran over her hands and the sight of it caused a smile to creep across her face. Erica had completely lost control and any semblance of rationality as she moved to and fro. She grabbed two zips ties that she'd purchased and restrained his legs to the chair. Then, she pulled the chair out away from the table so that Arnold was facing her and the foyer, twisting his hand awkwardly in doing so. The look that Erica had on her face almost made Arnold defecate on himself. He'd never seen her so deranged in all the years they had been together.

"Wait a minute, Erica. I don't know what you are planning but if you would just give me a minute to explain I'm sure that we can come to an understanding" pleaded Arnold.

Erica began circling him like a predator waiting to pounce on its prey. She looked down at him in disgust and contempt. What could he possibly say? Anything that would come from his mouth in that moment would be a lie with the goal of self-preservation. Just then, she decided she would entertain whatever he had to spill; it would only reinforce in her mind the legitimacy of her spilling his blood.

"Explain it all to me then Arnold, make me understand" she said mockingly.

"Okay... Okay..." began Arnold exasperated. "Samantha is an old friend of mine—"Arnold didn't get the chance to finish his sentence before Erica grabbed another knife from the table and sliced Arnold swiftly across the chest. Arnold screamed out in pain.

"If you start off telling another lie, the next stab will be a fatal one" Erica threatened as Arnold screamed bloody murder. He was so consumed by the excruciating pain he began fumbling to find the right words.

"Owwww.... okay... okay... it's all true Erica; Samantha, the kids, it's all true" he confessed. A part of Erica felt relieved by the revelations from Arnold, but they also enraged her.

"How could you, Arnold?" Erica pleaded. "After everything that we have been through, Arnold. You made me your wife, Arnold, I gave you a son, I gave you my world. Why, Arnold? Why didn't you just save me the pain and leave me a long time ago? Why go through all the trouble, why waste all the years just to throw it all away?" asked Erica, the hurt clear in her voice.

"It wasn't about hurting you or Arnold Jr." Arnold pleaded, panting.

"Then why, Arnold?" she asked.

Arnold grimaced from the pain that he was feeling. He felt himself becoming nauseous and he knew it was a result of massive blood loss. He told himself that so he needed to get Erica to calm down before she did something she would eventually regret. "I can't give you a reason, Erica. All I can do is admit my wrongs and provide you with whatever clarity it is that you need" Arnold paused briefly trying to regain his strength.

"Met Samantha during the time that we were going through the whole Kyle situation. It was during my trip to California that I confided in her about our problems. After I came back, we flew to London and I said that was all I needed from Samantha. As time passed, I found myself confiding in her more and more.... And I'm sure you can get the rest."

Erica looked at Arnold with hatred running all over her face. Swiftly, she brought the knife up and slashed him across the chest again, slicing him deeply. The pain caused Arnold to scream out again and blood splattered. "No, how about you tell me the rest" Erica angrily screamed.

"Okay... okay... Erica... trust me when I say I never intended for things to get this far out of control. The confiding led to sex, the sex led to a child" Arnold paused to regain his composure and gauging Erica's reaction to the last part. He knew that Erica would have been able to see past the infidelity, but not with the two children in the picture.

"From my understanding, our child wasn't your first. Do you know how much that hurts me? Not only did you give her your first child, you gave her another one. Once is a mistake, Arnold. Two, you were clearly playing house. You never planned to end it, Arnold. If she would have never shown her face today, we would still be living a lie."

Arnold's head shot from side to side searching for her. Standing behind him, she brought the knife to his neck, pinching the skin tightly.

"Erica, Erica, wait! I'm sorry, I promise you I am. I love you, Erica! I know that I made a mistake but my love for you and my child are genuine. Our marriage is real. I just got caught up, but I'm done with it, Erica, I promise you. All I want is our family."

Arnold's pleas did little to sway Erica. She began reminiscing on the visit she had from Samantha and Arnold's two children. Seeing the hurt in that poor woman's eyes showed her that she was just as oblivious to Arnold's deceit as she was and it angered Erica even more. It wasn't the cheating that she couldn't forgive, it was the duration of the affair and the children she couldn't forgive. A tear slowly slid down Erica's face and she quickly wiped it away. She didn't want to show any weakness or indecision as to what she planned to do. Slowly, she began to dig the knife deeper into Arnold's neck.

"I loved you so much, Arnold…" Erica began with tears in her eyes. "You made me believe in love again. I've always thought of you as my knight in shining armor— all the while you have been nothing but a liar, a cheater, and manipulator. This, I cannot forgive Arnold" stated Erica as she slowly began cutting Arnold's throat. Arnold began to gargle from the blood that was beginning to accumulate inside his esophagus, preventing him from begging Erica for mercy. Erica lost all control as she finished the job of cutting Arnold from ear to ear ending his life.

Conclusion

Eighteen months later, after sealing their union, Kyle and Zoe walked hand-in-hand down the aisle as rose petals were tossed above their heads courtesy of the wedding guests. Zoe had the biggest smile on her face while looking stunning in her custom Vera Wang gown. Kyle's smile matched hers as his eyes landed on his best friend and best man, Louis, who was with his wife

Cante in the crowd. Louis held Cante around the waist as a smile was also plastered on his face. Kyle took Zoe by the hand and led her to the makeshift dance floor that sat in the middle of the island. When they made their way down, they prepared themselves for their first dance together as husband and wife.

Once they were front and center on the dance floor, Zoe draped her arms around Kyle's neck, and he gently placed his hands on her hips as they danced. The attendees admired the beautiful couple as love filled the air. After finishing their first dance the rest of the reception joined them and danced to the possibility of forever.

"This is the happiest day of my life" said Kyle to Zoe while gazing into her eyes.

"Mine as well" Zoe replied lovingly.

"Can you believe that we've made it to this point?" asked Kyle.

"Honestly, I knew it from the day I first saw you on that plane with that sad look in your eyes. Believe it or not, I told myself then that one day you would be my husband" she said.

"Oh, so you felt like you just had it like that, huh?" Kyle teased.

"Well, yeah" replied Zoe confidently with a grin.

Together, they began to laugh at her bluntness. It had been a long journey. Kyle initially didn't believe it would go this far. It was his first time being in love after ending his relationship with Erica and it had him cautious. Now, here they stood as Mr. and Mrs. Kyle Malone and he had to admit that he was completely satisfied. After dancing to several songs, Kyle and Zoe made their way over to sit at the large round table that Big Momma was occupying as she slowly bounced the toddler on her knees.

"Big Momma, why didn't you get out there and dance?" asked Kyle.

"Because I had this Chilli to look after," replied Big Momma, in reference to Louis Johnson Jr. Just then, Cante and Louis joined them as Cante chimed in on the conversation. "What are y'all talking about?" asked Cante.

"Nothing much. I was just about to tell Kyle and Zoe how proud I am of them, but since the two of you are here as well, I might as well let you know how proud I am of all of you. Within y'all are true examples of what love and loyalty are. You have each been able to overcome the obstacles that have come your way and have remained faithful and true to one another through it. There will continue to be obstacles and hurdles which are simply opportunities to learn and become stronger together. You have to be in love with the struggles of being in love. Once you do, there will be nothing or no one that will be able to tear you apart. You must try your damndest to always be considerate of one another, to communicate with each other to provide encouragement and finally, to believe in the one you love. As long as you're able to accept the bad with the good, then you'll be alright" finished Big Momma.

"Thank you, Big Momma" replied the four in unison, just as Louis Jr. erupted in a fit of tears. Cante rose to her feet and made her way to Big Momma with her arms extended out for her son. "Give him to me," requested Cante to Big Momma.

"Chilli, go and sit back down. I got him, he's only fussing because he's not getting any attention, now you go ahead back over there with your husband" commanded Big Momma. Cante made it back over to Louis who sat there with a giant smile on his face.

"Thank you, Big Momma for always being available and bestowing upon us your wisdom, encouragement, and love. If it wasn't for you, I wouldn't know where I would be right now. So, thank you again, Big Momma" Kyle said affectionately as the rest of them echoed his sentiments.

"You don't have to thank me, Chilli, for doing what I'm supposed to be doing, but you can show your appreciation by going to retrieve me some of that punch, I'm quite parched" replied Big Momma. Kyle couldn't help but to laugh as he got up and made his way over to the punch bowl. He retrieved a cup as directed and began to pour Big Momma punch. A smile crept upon his face as he continued to think about the progression of his life. He was immeasurably fortunate to have Big Momma. He also felt that he was lucky to have Zoe as his wife. He felt fulfilled in his personal life and things were also great in his career as well.

After Alu was indicted and sentenced to five years in a federal prison at Terre Haute, Indiana, Precise Accounts flourished like it never had before. They were now the largest accounting firm in the states and third in the world. Yeah, life was indeed good.

"Congratulations" Kyle heard a familiar voice behind him. He turned and was face-to-face with Erica. His heart skipped a beat as it always seemed to do in her presence. "So, you made it, I see" replied Kyle after a moment.

"Yes, I did. Initially, I wasn't really sure I should come when I received the invitation, but after much consideration and constant pestering from Cante, I decided to attend. I must admit, you look really handsome and that wife of yours looks amazing. It's crazy because at one point in time I really believed that I would become Mrs. Malone," stated Erica seriously. Kyle paused while looking into Erica's eyes.

"Yeah, at one point in time I really thought the same thing, but I guess we can't control destiny or love's conclusion" replied Kyle.

"Yeah" replied Erica knowingly. A brief silence ensued as they tried finding the right words.

"So, I'm assuming your husband didn't come along with you" stated Kyle.

"My husband?" she replied.

"Yeah, Arnold," replied Kyle in confusion.

"Oh, I'm assuming Cante didn't tell you" she conceded.

"Cante don't tell me much about you these days" he said.

Erica didn't volunteer any information as she thought back on one of the last times that she saw Arnold….

Erica snapped back from her reverie of her killing Arnold as he looked over the table at her.

"Why are you acting so weird?" asked Arnold.

"I'm not acting weird, I'm just in shock at how you can sit in front of me and act as if everything in the world is fine" she replied.

"What are you talking about? Last I recall things are fine" he said.

"Well, clearly you are living in some kind of fantasy world" snapped Erica.

"Could you please stop speaking in riddles and explain to me just exactly what you are talking about?"

Erica looked over at Arnold with contempt and disgust. She really could not believe him and his manipulative ways. Rather than replying, she stood up from her chair and retrieved two envelopes. Once she made it back over to the table, she slid one of the envelopes in front of Arnold. Arnold picked up the envelope with a skeptical look in his eyes. He hesitated before opening the envelope and reviewing its contents. His heart dropped once the pictures came into his view. Him with Samantha, him with his kids, and finally the four of them as a family. Arnold's hands began to shake as he realized the gig was up. He attempted to speak and explain himself, but no words came out. He looked up into her eyes as she got done wiping a tear away.

"Erica, I'm sorry" stated Arnold.

"Is that all you have to say? That you are sorry?" she replied, resentful.

"I mean, I don't know what else there is to say. Apparently, you are very aware of what has been going on behind your back" he said.

"Tell me why, Arnold" she demanded.

"There really isn't a reason. I got caught up, Erica, and by the time I realized it, it was too late" he replied with regret.

"You deceived me, Arnold. You had me believing that our child was your first, but not only did you continue but you also have another child as well. Do you know how much that hurts Arnold?" Erica looked at Arnold and got the urge to do something extremely violent to him. She had so much contempt toward him at that moment, she couldn't believe how nonchalant he was behaving about such a serious breach of trust. Rather than exploding, Erica took the time to slide the other envelope over toward Arnold. Arnold picked up the second envelope and extracted the papers. Then, he began to read them. He realized he was reading the divorce papers.

"So, you want a divorce?" asked Arnold.

"Yes, I do. I don't want anything more to do with you. I'm requesting that you get fifty percent custody of your child and I do not want any of your assets or other alimony. I just want this all to go over quickly and smoothly and it can start by you getting your things and getting out of my house" finished Erica defiantly.

Arnold managed to chuckle aloud. "Never mind my things, you can get rid of it all. Again, I'm sorry Erica but this all was inevitable. Thank you for allowing this to end peacefully" finished Arnold coldly before he stood and retrieved his blazer and turned his back on Erica to walk away. Once Erica allowed her thoughts to come back to the present, she began to relay to Kyle everything that had transpired between her and Arnold, beginning with Samantha and the kids and ending with their divorce that had been officially finalized.

"So, where is Arnold now?" Kyle questioned.

"Well, last I heard he was in California with Samantha, I heard they were recently married and expecting child number three."

"I'm sorry that you had to go through all that," responded Kyle sincerely.

"All is fair in love and war, right?" replied Erica rhetorically.

Kyle simply nodded his head in agreement.

"So, how far along is she?" asked Erica concerning Zoe's baby bump.

"Five months, seventeen days and nine hours to be exact" replied Kyle while looking down at his Autamare Pigot.

"Still as meticulous as ever," replied Erica as they both burst into laughter. Just then, Zoe approached them.

"Babe, Big Momma is fussing about her punch. I think you need to get over there to give it to her" suggested Zoe before noticing Erica. "Oh, hey," she said to Erica.

"Hello" responded Erica.

"Zoe, this is Erica… and Erica, as you know, this is my wife, Zoe" introduced Kyle.

"OH!" replied Zoe. "This is the Erica that….?" asked Zoe. Kyle responded by simply nodding his head in affirmation.

"It's nice to finally meet you, Erica" replied Zoe.

"You too, and congratulations" stated Erica.

"Thank you" replied Zoe before focusing her attention back to Kyle. "Give me the punch, I'll take it back over to Big Momma before she has a fit," said Zoe while grabbing hold of the cup of punch from Kyle. "And don't be too long or I'll get lonely" finished Zoe as she turned and made her way back to Big Momma.

Once Zoe was out of earshot, Erica began to speak candidly. "She's very pretty" complimented Erica.

"Thank you" replied Kyle.

A brief silence ensued before Kyle asked, "Are you doing better now?"

"Actually, I am, I'm happier now than I have been in quite some time. I'm just trying to spend as much time with my son as possible and traveling whenever I'm free. I'm taking my time and enjoying my peace of mind."

"That's great" replied Kyle before another awkward silence ensued. "Well, let me get back out here before both Big Momma and Zoe lose their minds. Again, thank you for coming and as always it was very nice seeing you" finished Kyle.

"You too, " replied Erica as Kyle turned and headed back toward the reception. Before he made it back, Erica yelled out, "Kyle!" Kyle turned around to face her and with a smile on her face she told him "Take care of yourself."

"I will" replied Kyle before giving Erica his own best smile then turning and walking away.

The End

Live By It, Die By It (By: Ice Money)

Live By It, Die By It 2 (By: Ice Money)

Mercenary (By: Ice Money)

The Ruler of the Red Ruler (By: Kutta)

The Trenches: Murder, Money, Betrayal (By: Kutta)

Block Boyz (By: Juvi)

Da $treets Raised Me & Da Guns Paid Me (By Juvi & Splash Queen)

Team Savage (By: Ace Boogie)

Team Savage 2 (By: Ace Boogie)

Team Savage III (By: Ace Boogie)

Love Have Mercy (By: Kordarow Moore)

Rich Pride (By M.L. Moore)

Hittaz Die Every Day (By: Michael Lawrence)

Available at Bagzofmoneycontent.com and most major bookstores.

Made in the USA
Monee, IL
09 May 2022

96109981R10109